T0123427

Praise for *The Traitor's Niche*

"The quest for a rebel pasha's severed head becomes a grimly comic comment in John Hodgson's translation of this brilliant and laconic 1978 Albanian novel, an allegorical fable about 20th-century authoritarianism."
—*The New York Times Book Review*, Editors' Choice

"The book's political intentions are shrewd and unmistakable. By depicting the corruption and whimsical cruelty of the Ottoman Empire, Mr. Kadare smuggles in a damning appraisal of Albanian Communism . . . Its evocation of the past feels both contemporary (tourists flock to Istanbul to gawk at the severed head, and you can almost imagine them taking cellphone photos) and outside of time. Mr. Kadare has more in common with William Faulkner, a writer who spins mythology out of regional legends. This, too, is a moral project as well as an artistic one. In *The Traitor's Niche*, Mr. Kadare delineates the Ottoman Empire's efforts to vouchsafe subservience by expunging Albania of its language and customs. This unforgettable novel adds to his lifelong work of cultural reclamation. The past is uncannily present in his books—a phantom that walks among the living, or a severed head that seems to lock you in its gaze."
—*The Wall Street Journal*

"The novel relentlessly exposes the impact of authoritarianism, showing how it crushes the human spirit—including, perhaps most perniciously, the souls of those who aspire to be autocrats. Reading the book today, one can understand the response it provoked from the communist censors, since its critique, though displaced in time, is clearly directed at Hoxha's regime. Yet the story is also a more encompassing parable of authoritarianism that is relevant far beyond its immediate historical moment . . . Kadare also shows a unique talent at peering inside the mind of a tyrant . . . In *The Traitor's Niche*, as in all his best works, Kadare powerfully evokes—and critiques—the sheer, irascible strangeness of unchecked power." —*Los Angeles Review of Books*

"Finally (and very elegantly) translated . . . Riveting." —*The New York Times Book Review*

"Forty years after its publication in Albanian, the English translation by John Hodgson is effective in relaying the creative naturalism of his informal, though skillfully poetic, idiosyncratic tone . . . Kadare's fiction intuits the spirit of the art movements of his day, orbiting the dark ambiance of indie cinema, goth punk, shock installation. The gift of Kadare as a writer is also not merely in the aesthetics of his language, but in the rudimentary transmission of deft, witty meaning, and deeply satirical commentary." —MATT HANSON, *The Millions*

"Kadare's *Traitor's Niche* is a short, rich, thickly described indictment of empire, nationalism, and the state, a timely meditation on the violences of bureaucracy, corruption, and the injustice of justice." —*PopMatters*

"The baroque madness of the Ottoman bureaucracy is beautifully drawn, and the characters are sketched well. Each time you find yourself hoping against hope that you aren't meeting the next occupant of the niche."
—Historical Novel Society

"With its allegorical style, dark humor, and muscular commentary on contemporary Albania under Enver Hoxha, it is very much classic Kadare." —*Booklist*

"Kadare brilliantly examines the private cost of despotism while illustrating a crucial episode in the history of Albania. Kadare's powerful, nimble novel is a gem."
—*Publishers Weekly*

"A political fable of decapitation amid totalitarian oppression combines wickedly funny satire with darker, deeper lessons . . . The only signs that it's set in the early 19th century are offhand references to Byron and Napoleon; otherwise it reads less like historical fiction than timeless prophecy, as it anticipates the relentless expansion of an empire."
—*Kirkus Reviews*

"This piercingly beautiful work quietly delivers a persuasive sense of human violence." —*Library Journal*

Ismail Kadare

THE TRAITOR'S
NICHE

A Novel

*Translated from the Albanian
by John Hodgson*

COUNTERPOINT
BERKELEY, CALIFORNIA

The Library of Congress has catalogued the hardcover as follows:
Names: Kadare, Ismail, author. | Hodgson, John, 1951– translator.
Title: The traitor's niche : a novel / Ismail Kadare ; translated from the
    Albanian by John Hodgson.
Other titles: Kamarja e turpit. English
Description: Berkely, CA : Counterpoint Press, 2018. | "First published
    with the title Kamarja e Turpit in 1978 by Naim Frashri Publishing
    House, Tirana" — ECIP galley.
Identifiers: LCCN 2017055406 | ISBN 9781640090446
Subjects: LCSH: Albanian fiction—Translations into English. | Turkey—
    History—Ottoman Empire, 1288–1918—Fiction. | Albania—
    History—Fiction. | GSAFD: Historical fiction.
Classification: LCC PG9621.K3 K3413 2018 | DDC 891/.9913—dc23
LC record available at https://lccn.loc.gov/2017055406

Paperback ISBN: 978-1-64009-202-0

COUNTERPOINT
2560 Ninth Street, Suite 318
Berkeley, CA 94710
www.counterpointpress.com

Printed in the United States of America

THE TRAITOR'S NICHE

I

At the Center of the Empire

THE UNBLINKING eyes met the stares of the passersby
and tourists who poured into the square from all directions. The tourists' own gaze, like that of all moving crowds,
was mild and unfocused, but people's eyes suddenly froze
as soon as they encountered this sight, as if their astonished
pupils struggled to sink back into the depths of their skulls,
and only the impossibility of doing this compelled them to
stand still and face what they saw. Most went pale, some
wanted to vomit. Only a few looked on calmly. The eyes
were indifferent, of a color you could not call bluish or even
gray, and which it was hard to name, because it was less a
color than the distant reflection of a void.

Looking away at last, the clusters of tourists would ask how
to get to Hagia Sophia, to the tombs of the sultan-emperors,
the bank, the old bathhouses, the Palace of Dreams. They
inquired hurriedly and feverishly, yet most did not leave the
square but wandered around as if caught in a trap. Although
not particularly large, the square was one of the most famous
in the ancient imperial capital. Paved with green granite,

it appeared to be cast in bronze, and its splendor was yet further enhanced by the metal lions' heads behind the railings enclosing the Central State Archive. Above the wing of the Archive peered not only the lead-tipped minaret of the Sultan's Mosque, but also the Obelisk of Tokmakhan, brought over a few centuries ago to commemorate the invasion of Egypt, and decorated with hieroglyphs and the different emblems of the empire all cast in metal, and finally the Cannon Gate, in whose walls was carved the Traitor's Niche. In the language of the country, this niche was called the stone of *ibret*, a word that might loosely be translated as "deterrence."

It was not hard to imagine why this square had been chosen for the niche where the severed heads of rebel viziers or ill-starred senior officials were placed. Perhaps nowhere else could the eyes of passersby so easily grasp the interdependency between the imposing solidity of the ancient square and the human heads that had dared to show it disrespect. It was clear at once that the niche had been sited in the wall to convey the impression that the head's lifeless eyes surveilled every corner of the square. In this way, even the feeblest and least imaginative passerby could visualize, at least for a moment, his own head displayed at this unnatural height.

When the head's hair fluttered forlornly in the wind, the contrast between those soft wisps and the solid monuments of the square, especially the lions' manes, was a sight beyond endurance.

The square had an extraordinary solemnity, metal and

stone coming together everywhere. Even on the terrace of the café opposite, metal was present in the copper utensils used for the fragile and human act of drinking coffee.

The former government news-criers who had now retired due to age or professional incapacity, having lost their voices, were among those who usually came here to drink coffee. The café owner told Abdulla, the keeper of the Traitor's Niche, how their conversation was restricted entirely to old news and the decrees they had once proclaimed to every corner of the state.

In the morning, before the square came to life, Abdulla liked to observe the café. After his working hours, he also liked to sit at one of the little tables, but rarely did so, because the doctor had told him that coffee was bad for his health. Abdulla was thirty-one years old, but there was no strength in his lanky limbs. At times, a ringing in his ears drained him of all energy. Like everything else on this square, the coffee was too potent. Despite this, Abdulla risked a cup now and then. On these occasions he preferred to join the table of the old news-criers. In the past their voices had made glass windows shake, but now only a pitiful squeak emerged from their throats. The café owner said he could easily understand why they considered the decrees of yesteryear more impressive than those of today, just as they themselves had outshone the modern criers. The café owner said that the criers, almost without exception, could remember the day they had lost their voices, and not just the day, but the decree they were issuing, and the very phrase at which their vocal cords had given out forever. "That's what people are like," he went on bitterly. "They never forget anything."

Watching the swarm of people, Abdulla felt sure that the café owner was right and that people deserved the shock that the niche gave them. He knew that the sight of a severed head was not something everybody could stomach, but Abdulla always found that the horror and distress in the spectators' faces went beyond all expectation. It was the eyes in the head that seemed to strike them most, and not because they were dead eyes, but perhaps because people were accustomed to human eyes making an impression on them when connected to a human body with arms and legs. Abdulla thought that the absence of a body made the eyes larger and more significant than they really were.

Indeed, it seemed to Abdulla that people in general were less significant than they thought themselves to be. Sometimes, when dusk drew near and the moon cast its light prematurely on the square, he even thought that human beings, himself included, were only a pollutant that spoiled the splendor and harmony of the imperial square. He could not wait for the square to empty entirely so that, although his official working hours were over, he could observe everything in the calm, icy moonlight. Sometimes the light fell at a certain angle on the niche and for an instant the illuminated head would assume a derisive or disdainful expression. The head, now free of human limbs, seemingly useless appendages, appeared slightly worthier of taking its place among the ancient symbols and emblems of the square. At these moments, Abdulla would be seized by a thrilling paroxysm of self-destruction, an obscure subconscious desire to throw off the ungainly tangle of his limbs and become only a head.

During the day, Abdulla's face wore a permanently rigid expression. This was fitting as long as he was on duty. In a way, he was forced to adapt himself to the stony aspect of the square. He was the keeper of one of its most important symbolic sites, and he had to look the part. However, although Abdulla stood only a few paces from the niche and it was obvious that he and he alone was in charge of it, nobody took any notice of him. Everybody's eyes were fixed in wonder on the niche. Abdulla felt a faint spasm of jealousy, as if this feeling were mixed in a huge pot with all kinds of other emotions.

For the thousandth time he looked at all the features of the square in turn, as if to measure, should he be counted as one of them, how far he fell short of the necessary perfection. Only the hieroglyphs on the Egyptian obelisk were on a similarly diminutive scale and less than majestic. They resembled insects that had become petrified while crawling up the pillar. Sometimes, when he did not feel well, it seemed to Abdulla that the hieroglyphs had suddenly come to life and started to move, as if trying to wriggle free from the grip of stone and metal and set off like nomads towards the desert. But this happened rarely, and only when he was particularly exhausted. Still more rare were his moments of extreme weakness when he thought of escaping in the same way, like a beetle, out of this granite vice.

It was morning, and crowds of pedestrians and tourists flooded the square from all directions, from the Street of Islamic Arms, the crossroads where the Obelisk of Tokmakhan stood, and the adjacent Crescent Square. Abdulla carefully studied their behavior. One bold tourist came very close to the niche. His furrowed brow and the strained concentration in his eyes suggested that he was trying to read the inscription underneath, which Abdulla knew by heart: "This is the head of the vizier Bugrahan Pasha, condemned by the Sovereign Sultan, dishonored in war and defeated by Ali Pasha Tepelena, former governor of Albania and traitor to the Empire."

The clock in the neighboring Crescent Square struck ten. Abdulla walked a few paces towards the niche and leaned a wooden ladder against the wall. He felt the crowd behind his back go still in expectation as he slowly climbed its rungs. The spectators broke into a murmur of horror and wonder. There were whispers: "What is he doing? What is he doing?" This was one of the finest moments of the day, when at last he became the center of attention. He had no right to do anything to the head, not even to touch it. His task was merely to inspect its general condition, and to inform the doctor at once of anything unusual.

Avoiding the head's eyes as always, Abdulla spent a few moments studying the shallow copper dish on which the head stood, its neck resting in a layer of honey. The cold was tightening its grip, and the honey had frozen. Abdulla, with his back turned to the crowd, carefully descended the ladder. The whispers of "What did he do? What did he do?" gradually subsided, and he resumed his place. The passersby and tourists looked at him with respect, but not for long; soon a new wave of people came who had not witnessed his inspection, and Abdulla was again ignored. This routine was repeated at four o'clock in the afternoon. According to the regulations, the head had to be examined twice a day in winter and four times in summer. It was more difficult in the hot weather, when he had to scatter chunks of ice and salt in the copper dish and report to the doctor each day, instead of twice a week as in the winter.

At the end of the previous summer, the difficult first summer of his duty, there had been a general inspection of the square. Those had been days of real anxiety for him. Several times he'd thought he was on the point of losing his job, or worse. The commission of government inspectors was strict. The keeper of the Obelisk of Tokmakhan had been sentenced to life imprisonment because a rust stain was found on the left side of its western face, an inch above the ground. Three other keepers were dismissed, and the cleaner of the iron lions was sentenced to have his right hand broken because the granite slab beneath the lions was encrusted with mold. The commission had stood for a long time in front of the Traitor's Niche, which at that time held the head of the rebel vizier of Trebizond. They tried to find some pretext to accuse the doctor and the keeper of not complying with *Reg-*

ulations for the Care of Heads, and asked devious questions about the unnaturally yellow tinge of the vizier's face and the lack of eye color. Abdulla had been struck speechless, but the doctor courageously defended himself, and said that the vizier's complexion, even in life, had been sallow, as is typical of men with rebellion and treason in their blood. As for the lack of color in the eyes (which had in fact obviously begun to decompose), the doctor quoted the old saying that the eyes are a window to the soul: it would be useless to look for color in the eyes of a man who had never had a soul. The doctor's explanations were hardly convincing, not to say vacuous, but for this very reason they were hard to argue with. The inspectors were obliged to withdraw their remarks and the matter concluded with a mere reprimand and a warning of dismissal for Abdulla.

The business with the vizier of Trebizond's head seemed to Abdulla a bad omen for his career, and he was only heartened when the head was removed from the niche and replaced with that of the thirty-seven-year-old governor Nuri Pasha—or the "blond pasha," as he had been known in his lifetime, due to the slightly pale color of his hair and skin. After his working hours that evening, Abdulla had sat down in the café opposite for the first time. The proprietor, who recognized him and welcomed him with respect, had a slightly yellowish complexion, with narrow eyes and veins in his temples that swelled whenever he approached with the coffeepot in his hand. His conversation flowed as naturally from his mouth as the coffee trickled from the spout of the pot. "People are villains, there's no improving them," he said to Abdulla, pouring the coffee. Later Abdulla heard him use the same words to open conversation with almost everyone. Some people indicated they didn't want to listen or gave him such a frosty expression that the café owner said no more. But others encouraged him with some remark, and he would continue. The stream from the copper spout ceased, but not the one from his mouth. He went on talking to Abdulla: "People are villains. They look at the severed head as if the sight of it has put them off ever committing a crime again, but as soon as they turn their backs on it, it's clear they can hardly wait to get back to their dirty tricks."

Ever since that first evening, Abdulla had noticed a kind of congruence between the copper pot and the café owner's physiognomy. The pot reflected something in his face, either the color of his skin or the arch of his nose. Or perhaps it was the other way around, and his face over the years had begun to resemble the copper coffeepot. Encouraged by a glance from Abdulla, the café owner continued: "Otherwise, people would have learned a lesson from all those heads in that niche of shame." The café owner sat down for a while at his table, and said that he had been friendly with Abdulla's two predecessors. Abdulla knew that the niche had been inaugurated only a few years before, and the café owner remembered the precise day and hour. He even recalled exactly when the imperial palace staff had first appeared in the square, bustling about, taking measurements and setting up markers. He remembered the arrival of two masons and their first mallet blows against the Cannon Gate's ancient wall. At that time nobody, not even the workmen themselves, knew why they were gouging out this cavity. The secret was kept even after the work was finished, and indeed until the morning of that unforgettable winter day (it was December, just like now, the café owner added) when dawn broke to reveal a human head in the stone niche. It was December, the café owner repeated, and snow was falling. The head had gray hair. The snow swirled around the square and it seemed as if the head and the sky were tossing flakes to and fro.

Abdulla remembered that it was precisely at this time that he had first heard the word *independence*. The word had now become fashionable, and he even noticed it in the rapid speech of foreign tourists. The niche had been inaugurated at a time when independence attempts had redoubled. The old chronicles in the State Archive were full of provincial rebellions, but these had become particularly frequent in recent years. The empire was the most powerful state of the time; a "superstate," as its enemies called it, encompassing three continents, twenty-nine peoples, six religions, four races, and forty languages. With such a jumble of tongues it was natural for entire areas of the state to be in rebellion, like that old troublemaker, Albania, which had been up in arms for the past year. Its governor, Ali Tepelena, the most powerful of all imperial viziers, had finally thrown off his mask and gone to war after a quarter-century of covert disobedience to his sovereign. Abdulla had often overheard and even shared stories about rebellions, but it had never crossed his mind that the day would come when he would be appointed keeper of the Traitor's Niche, which symbolized in an extraordinary way everything that could be said or thought about the independence of peoples, and which inspired such horror.

The nearby clock struck eleven. The square was almost full, and among the crowd, whose continual eddying made one dizzy, Abdulla made out the doctor advancing towards him with vigorous strides. It was the day of his regular weekly visit.

"Good morning, Abdulla!" the doctor said cheerfully.

"Good morning!"

"How are things?" the doctor asked, raising his eyes to the niche. "When's the wedding?"

"Next week," Abdulla said, feeling himself blush.

"Oho," exclaimed the doctor. "Not long now." He rubbed his hands together with glee. "Shall we take a look at this lover boy?"

"As you wish," said Abdulla, and went to fetch the wooden ladder. The guards, with spears in their hands, observed the crowd out of the corners of their eyes. The doctor nimbly climbed the ladder, set down his bag in a corner of the recess, and inspected the head. He pressed it with deft fingers: first the temples, then under the eyes and on the throat, while whistling all the time under his breath. Then he opened his bag, took out a bottle and a piece of cotton, moistened the cotton with the liquid from the bottle, and carefully dabbed the head in all the places where he had touched it. Then he took out a smaller bottle, and with the help of a pipette squeezed several drops of liquid into the corners of both eyes. When he had finished, he returned the bottles and the remaining cotton to the bag and, after wiping away the last drops of moisture and fragments of cotton from one hardened cheek, patted the other lightly, almost affectionately, as if to say, amazing, no problems here at all.

"A miracle," he said aloud, cheerfully waving his hand as he descended. "Goodbye for now, Abdulla."

Abdulla followed him with his eyes as he vanished among the crowd of people. The grimmest and most doleful expression in the world would have surprised Abdulla less than this levity of the doctor.

The drowsy hubbub of the square filled Abdulla's ears, and now and then there rose, like flecks of foam to the surface of the sea, fragments of words and phrases. Abdulla stood like a rock washed by this chatter, which flowed into the hollows of his eyes, down his cheeks, through his beard, drenching him like a rainstorm . . . Whose is this head? . . . head . . . whose . . . this head . . . it belonged to General . . . Gen . . . Bugrahan Pasha . . . Gen . . . defeated by Ali Pasha . . . and why have they put it . . . why . . . put . . . why in . . . of the Traitor's . . . Niche . . . how . . . because he lost the war . . . But this Ali . . . this pasha . . . Ali Tepelena . . . what did you say? The rebel pasha of the province of Albania? . . . Where is this province? . . . Oh, a long way . . . Haven't you read the newspapers? On the edge of the empire . . . the edge . . . the cursed frontier of the empire . . . What do they call it in their own language? . . . *Shqi . . . Shqip . . . Shqipëria* . . . I can't hear you because of the noise . . . What a name . . .

This province must really be far, Abdulla thought. His elder brother had been sent there on duty this past summer, and still no letter had arrived from him. Whenever the name of Albania was mentioned on the square, which happened often because of the current head, he involuntarily thought of a bloody rib of horsemeat he had once seen in a market when he was a child. A long way, he said to himself again. Distant and unruly. Tavdja Tokmakhan, the legendary hero of the Janissaries, in whose memory the obelisk had been raised in the square, had also been killed there four hundred years ago. It was truly a cursed country.

The muffled roar of the square engulfed him. Neither fear nor the bitter winter cold ever stopped people's talk. Words, wreathed in vapor, as if trying somehow to veil themselves, blithely flew from human mouths. Then these same mouths, which had committed such dangerous sins, blew on red, chilblained hands, while the eyes assumed an innocent expression. These people talked about the cursed frontier of the empire. Some believed it was to the west and some to the north, while most had no idea where it might be. Some people expressed the view that everything that happened on the state's periphery was always bad, and there should be no mercy for anybody. "Certainly there will be no mercy," a man replied, pretending to be in the know, and another

15

man asked if this meant the sultan himself would go . . . like when . . . "I didn't say anything of the sort and never mentioned the sultan," the first man retorted. "I was only talking about mercy." But the other man insisted: "When you talk about the sultan, you inevitably think of mercy."

Stark mad, Abdulla thought to himself. To block his ears to their ramblings, he tried to catch other voices. There was talk about fluctuations in the stock exchange and the falling price of gold, tests of new weapons that were expected to take place during this very conflict, and a predicted reshuffle in the War Ministry. A tourist was saying to his friends that the Imperial Bank's exchange rate, and even the number of tourist visas issued by the embassies, depended directly on the outcome of this war.

Abdulla suddenly sensed that a gap had opened up in the usual din of the square. It held for a few moments before it was filled by whispers and murmured inquiries of "Who's this?" that flowed into it like water, and then the rumbling of carriage wheels. Abdulla heard a scatter of voices saying, "Halet, the high official," "Halet is passing through," and he stood on tiptoe for a better view. The carriage of the senior state dignitary passed by a few paces from him.

Abdulla could not tear his eyes away from that long face, under whose fine skin bluish veins were visible. The official's eyes, veiled behind a curtain of total indifference, and the way he leaned against the back of his seat, set him entirely apart from the crowd, all curiosity, which swarmed around him.

Abdulla remembered what the doctor had once said, that

there were some people whose blood did not clot easily. In these cases, you have to add special substances, not exactly defined in the regulations, to the honey in which the head is placed. The doctor complained about the regulations. He kept saying that it was time to reconsider them in the light of recent medical knowledge.

To have to deal with heads like that would be the last straw, Abdulla thought as he watched the carriage disappear on the opposite side of the square. He felt almost certain that the blue-veined head of Halet the official was one of this kind.

"He was the one who collected the complaints against Ali Pasha of the Albanians and drew up the final report for the sultan," said a voice close to Abdulla's right ear.

Abdulla remembered well the public announcement of the uprising of the Albanian pasha and the effect of the news on the capital city. That same day, a proclamation changed Ali Pasha's name to Kara Ali, meaning "Black Ali," and an imperial order to crush the rebellion was issued. He remembered the whispers in the streets and the cafés, especially among artists and intellectuals, with that light in their eyes, a feverish glitter that appeared whenever there was trouble in the empire.

Shortly after Halet passed by, Abdulla sensed that the crowd in the square had changed, as new voices repeated the same questions: Whose head is that? Why? Where is Albania? Hurshid Pasha is fighting there now. The price of bronze, tourist visas . . .

The square was like a swimming pool whose water changed every half hour. Its churning noise was narcotic: Halet the official . . . he was a real troublemaker. The bronze price will go up again . . . bronze, *nz, z . . . zz . . .*

Abdulla turned his eyes to the niche. The head of Ali Tepelena, the pasha of Albania, would have to go there soon. The glorious Hurshid Pasha had set off to capture it. All the newspapers were writing about him. He had either to bring back the rebel's head or relinquish his own, like the ill-fated Bugrahan, two months ago. When Bugrahan Pasha left for Albania, the niche had been empty. The first winter frosts appeared. The hole that gaped in the wall seemed hungry. It had been waiting for Ali Pasha, that rare visitor to the capital, but in its place had come the head of the defeated Bugrahan, cut off by order of the sovereign. The niche now waited again, indifferently, for either Black Ali or the glorious Hurshid, the sultan's favorite.

Perhaps for the thousandth time, Abdulla looked at the head. Because of a slight angle of the sword at the moment of execution, or because of the physical build of the victim, it seemed a little slanted to one side. Abdulla clearly remembered Bugrahan Pasha setting off for war. Now it seemed to him that even then the vizier, astride his magnificent horse, had held his head at a slight angle. The military music echoing round the square, the banners above the Cannon Gate and the Obelisk of Tokmakhan, the high state dignitaries who had come out to see off the vizier, the pupils of the religious schools with flowers in their hands, the farewell speeches—

all these things were fixed in Abdulla's memory. But above all he could not put out of his mind the last moment before Bugrahan departed, when, waving his hand to the cheering crowds, he had turned his head towards the niche and averted his eyes at once. It had seemed to Abdulla that the vizier's features had clenched in a grimace. Two months later, before dawn on the first Wednesday of December, when the doctor and two protocol officials brought the head of the defeated Bugrahan, the first thing to flash through Abdulla's mind was the image of that brief glance towards the empty niche.

The clock on the neighboring square struck noon. The café opposite was full of people. The cold was tightening its grip. Abdulla thought that from where he stood he could sense the melancholy mood of the section of the clientele described by the doctor as "the old state criers in their grief." Abdulla knew that if he drank strong coffee there, with a little hashish, his eyes would view differently this crowd that endlessly whirled and seethed within the square's granite perimeter. He had tried this several times. Before his eyes, the crowd had turned into a mass of heads and bodies, whose furious gestures suggested that they were impatient to cut themselves asunder from one another. Their quarrel must be as old as the world itself. At such moments Abdulla was thankful for the invention of all the necklaces and chains, scarves and helmet straps with which people kept their heads firmly fastened to their bodies. All these had been devised to prevent heads from being detached. But he noticed that the more splendid this neckwear appeared, and the thicker its gold embroidery (depending on its wearer's position in the state hierarchy), the more the head and body were inclined to come apart. Usually when his train of thought reached this point, Abdulla's hand went involuntarily to his own neck with its ordinary shirt collar, and this movement of his hand was accompanied by a feeling of despair as shallow and insipid as everything else in his life.

2

On the Empire's Frontier

OST OF Albania's rebellious southern pashadom was
under snow. Yet the landscape was not uniformly
white, but broken up by dark patches and cracks caused by
the jagged terrain. The lowlands lay black under the freezing
wind. The snow and the land were both old, and knew each
other's wiles.

The land of the Albanians had been part of the Ottoman
Empire for four hundred years. The empire had ancient territories dating back almost eight hundred years, as well as very
recent additions. Now winter had come to all of them: to
the old domains of the imperial heartland, or Dar-al-Islam,
as they were called, and to the new possessions—known
as the Dar-al-Harb, which might be translated as "foreign
lands" or "lands of war"; to the great renegade pashadoms, to
the regions put to sleep after losing their nationhood, to the
regions that enjoyed privileges—or the halal lands, as they
were once called; to the snowfields, to the treacherous shad-
owlands where the sun never penetrated, and to the marshes
made all the more desolate by the clamor of geese. In short,

to all the provinces whose stations and destinies had been laid down in the recent special decree, "On the Status of the Empire."

Only clouds, mists, rainbows, winds, rains, and the royal messengers on the muddy highways roamed freely from one part of the mighty state to another. As winter approached, there had been more couriers than ever.

The winter was harshest on the frontier of the empire, and especially in the land of the Albanians. Or perhaps it seemed this way because of the rebellion. It had been apparent for many years that conflicts increased the heat when they occurred in summer, but had the opposite effect in winter, when the wind cut more sharply than a sword.

This was Albania's second major uprising since its sub-jugation. Throughout the autumn, it was rumored in the capital city that the sultan-emperor himself would march against the distant territory, just like at the time of Scan-derbeg's great rebellion. This plan was considered to have good and bad aspects. The good was obvious, in that it was clear to everybody that a campaign led by the sover-eign himself would quickly suppress the uprising. The bad was that an imperial offensive stuck in the memory and, unlike in previous times, the capital increasingly set store by forgetting.

It was previously thought that states had so many memo-rials and monuments in order that nothing should be for-gotten. But it was discovered later that a major state had as much need to forget as to remember, if not more. The memories of events and statesmen paled as the years passed. Dust covered them, mud stained them, until they were finally erased as if they had never been. But recently people had come to understand that forgetting was more difficult and complicated than remembering. It was forbidden, for example, to mention the name of Scanderbeg in books or the press, but there was no such ruling regarding the two sultans' campaigns against him in Albania. Nobody dared say that poems and chronicles could no longer mention the sovereigns' battles. But at the same time, nobody could advise how to answer bothersome questions: who had the great emperors set off to fight against, and what had they done when they arrived?

The Central Archive could perform many miracles, as it had done with the Balkans, but it was beyond its skill to hide these looming questions that emerged through the fog like mountaintops and seemed to glint above the entire world.

Albania had rebelled many times since the death of Scanderbeg, may he never rest in peace, but never like this. This was an extended rebellion that came in waves like the shocks of an earthquake, sometimes overtly, sometimes in secret. It had been started long ago by the old Bushatli family in the north and continued by Ali Pasha Tepelena in the south, and was shaking the foundations of the historic empire.

During the long autumn, everybody in the capital talked about the Albanian affair. Obviously, the rebel territory would be severely punished, and the era of the great pashadoms in Albania would come to an end. But this was not enough for the old aristocratic and religious elites. They wanted to know why matters had been allowed to go so far, and who was to blame. For years they had opposed the favors shown to Albania. They had written letters and issued warnings. But the rot had not been stopped.

Instead, something unprecedented had happened. For forty years, the great native pashas of Albania, Kara Mahmud Bushatli in the north and Ali Tepelena in the south, had kept the country beyond the reach of the Sublime Porte. They said that Kara Mahmud, the pasha of the north, rushed out like a tiger from the ravines of his frontier domain at whim and attacked neighboring states without the permission of the capital, breaking all the alliances, treaties, and agreements that had been reached with so much effort, and turning the state's entire foreign policy upside down. The foreign minister, the Reiz Efendi, appeared before the sultan, rending his cheeks and beard, and demanded that either this rampaging pasha be put in his place, or he himself should be dismissed.

"Kara Mahmud Bushatli, a model civil servant," the British consul, famous for his quips, had once said. If he was not mistaken, this pasha had waged war on neighboring states six times without the sultan's permission. He had been pronounced a traitor on each occasion and sentenced to death, but was always pardoned. The seventh time he had attacked a foreign country, again without permission, and he had been killed there. Oh God, such pashas existed only in the

Balkans. And just look at his name: Kara Mahmud, with that handle, *Kara*, meaning "Black," attached by the official curse. Apparently he'd liked the sobriquet, and besides, he was aware that after every pardon he would be condemned again, so he kept it joined to his name, rather as we hesitate to put down a wet hood when we come in from the rain, knowing that we are going straight out again.

People laughed at the Englishman, although everyone knew that the European consuls were, without exception, embroiled in the business of both Kara Mahmud and Ali Pasha. Carriages bearing their diplomatic crests swept through the renegade pashadoms like the north wind. But to the consuls' surprise, apart from its besieged castles the vast province of Albania was to all appearances at peace. With their faces glued to the little windows of their coaches, they expected to see turmoil and bloodshed, but found only silence. They referred to their newspapers, as if trying to confirm from the headlines that there was indeed an uprising, and poked their heads outside, but everywhere there was the same desolation. It was as though the noise and mayhem had been projected to the royal capital, while here at its source everything was frozen in silence.

Newspaper headlines reported to all corners of the state that Ali Tepelena, governor of Albania, a seven-times-decorated pasha and member of the Council of Ministers, proclaimed by royal decree as Kara Ali, meaning "Black Ali," was besieged in his last fortress. Hurshid Pasha, the army's rising star and the emperor's favorite, was suppressing the rebellion, and had refused all meetings with journalists and consuls.

On the fourth of February, the French consul's carriage was traveling past the encampment of a unit of the besieging army. From deep inside the camp came the sound of festive drumming. The consul stretched his head out the window to ask what all this pounding was about. "The *hayir ferman*," several voices replied from the semidarkness. "What?" the consul asked. "What's that?" "It's the decree pardoning Ali Pasha's life," someone replied. "The war's over."

How was this possible, the consul wondered, and stretched his head out of the carriage to ask more questions, but around him there was only dusk and spoiled snow. How was this possible, he wondered again. The whole world was waiting for Ali Pasha's severed head. In the capital, there were people who kept vigil all night by the Traitor's Niche, and curses against the black vizier had been sung from the empire's hundred thousand minarets. How could it all come to this ordinary end?

It was totally dark outside. The snow now looked black, and the French consul, wrapped in his fur-lined cloak, racked his brain to think of what he would report to his king.

They must come now, thought Hurshid Pasha for perhaps the hundredth time. He paced from one end of the tent to the other with long strides, and as he walked he shifted his rings from one trembling finger to the next. They must come now, he almost cried aloud. He thought he heard footsteps, and listened. But it was not footsteps, only the rustling of his robe, which stopped as soon as he stood still.

No more gunshots or shouts of war were audible. It seemed that everything was over, and still they hadn't come. For an instant, he imagined them walking towards him with heavy feet, like in a nightmare. Hurry up a little, for God's sake, he appealed silently. But their feet stuck as if in dough. The script of the sultan's decree, which Ali Pasha perhaps held in his hands, flashed in front of his eyes. That decree pardoned the empire's greatest rebel . . . but the sultan's signature strangely resembled a scorpion with its poisonous sting pointing upward. The decree was false. Ali would be beheaded as soon as he surrendered.

Then why . . . ? He left his thought unfinished. Involuntarily he reached out his arm for support. His knees buckled. They were coming. He could hear their footsteps. They were footsteps of a particular kind, neither hurried nor slow. One could not tell from what direction they came, but it was as if they were descending from some height or climbing from deep down. Their sound gave no indication of what news they brought, joyful or bitter. His arm, still searching for support, flailed in the air like a stork's wing. At that moment they entered. Hurshid Pasha's eyes fixed on a point about three feet above the ground, exactly where their hands should be. He did not look at any of their faces. He saw only that white thing that one of them held. The silver basin glittered. There was a head in it. No, it wasn't a head, but a fairy-tale lantern whose fire illuminated the entire world. Allah, he said to himself and raised his hands to his face, protecting his eyes from this blazing light.

"Pasha," the man holding the silver dish broke the silence. "Here is the head of Black Ali."

Hurshid Pasha stretched out his arms towards it, but instantly pulled them back. His hands would not hold that radiant dish. With an effort, he averted his eyes from it, and with the same awkwardness pointed to the little table in the middle of the tent. The man holding the dish bowed his head in a gesture of obedience, went to the table, and placed the dish upon it.

"Leave now," Hurshid Pasha said in a voice like the slenderest of threads. Two or three more words and it would snap.

The men went out in silence. Hurshid Pasha stood petrified in the middle of the tent, waiting for movement to come back to his body. Life returned first to his legs. Like the legs of a small child, they carried him unsteadily towards the table. For a while he stood numb beside the table, and then bent down over the silver dish and, holding it carefully in trembling hands, kissed the severed head. His shoulders heaved with sobbing. His hands, with cramped fingers frozen, stroked the woolly curls. Feverishly he watched the gems of his rings as they dived and surfaced among the white locks as if through winter clouds, and again his shoulders shook.

"My pasha," he said. "My guiding star."

He bent down and kissed the head again, then stepped

back to examine it more carefully. Here it is, he thought, on this dish, on this table, in my tent. It was really there, two paces from him. For months it had been as far from his grasp as a clap of thunder.

For entire days and nights during those grim weeks as the war and the siege continued, he had thought of this head. Like all things to do with infinity, its image would not settle in his mind. It was always distant, sometimes brooding or threatening, but mostly inscrutable.

He stroked the head again, but the glint of his rings next to the lifeless eyes was so frightening that he drew back his hands.

"My savior," he said, his voice breaking. "My destiny."

Ever since he had been appointed commander-in-chief of the troops to suppress the rebellion, it had seemed to Hurshid Pasha that the head of Black Ali hovered above the horizon of his life like a star in the sky. It was his duty to quench its light or be snuffed out himself. The heavens could not contain them both. One of their suns had to sink.

Throughout those weeks of war, the possibility of losing his own head had tortured him. On overcast mornings, every ache in his neck struck him as an ominous sign. Whenever he looked in the mirror, he could not help thinking of what would happen to his head, or to the other head, that of his double. This head, too, had teeth and a beard, and made speeches and issued orders like every head that commands an army. They had many things in common, but not their fate. One of them would inevitably fall. At moments of exhaustion and weakness, when it seemed that it would be difficult to defeat the legendary pasha of the Albanians, he had been haunted by listless fantasies. How good it would be if customs could change and become gentler, so that the world would accept both of them, the victor and the vanquished. But even in his sluggish dreams this seemed impossible. It was easier to imagine himself with two heads on his shoulders, his own and Ali's—or worse, their heads at either end of his body, one below and one above. In fact it was easier to imagine any kind of monstrosity than to consider the prospect of them both living on the same earth.

All these fantasies now belonged to the past. This head was in front of him, its light extinguished forever on that February afternoon. So why did he feel no joy at all? The exultation was all around him, and he had only to reach out to share in it, but something stopped him. What's wrong with you, he said to himself. His star has set, yours is rising. What more do you want?

Nothing, he thought after a moment, but then the reason why he couldn't rejoice occurred to him. He was afraid. It was no longer the authentic fear for his own head that had been so familiar to him in the past few weeks. It was a more pervasive, mute terror that went down to the foundations of the earth. He had witnessed with his own eyes a mighty fall. He had seen majesty brought low. Yet his own joy squirmed like a squashed worm. His feelings were cold. The worm went still. Why did it have to happen like this?

The chill penetrated his bones. It was the same iciness that he had felt the previous night, when, having withdrawn to his tent, he'd listened to the din of the drums. They were celebrating the arrival of what they took to be the royal *hayir ferman*, pardoning Ali Pasha. Half-crazed dervishes, with faces blue, danced and fell prostrate, foaming, while around them thousands of soldiers, elated at the end of the campaign, clapped their hands. Nobody knew that the *ferman* was false. The true decree, the *katil ferman*, which the messenger kept sewn into his jacket, would be revealed to Ali only at the last moment before his death.

All this was over. Hurshid Pasha walked slowly to the entrance of his tent. Dusk was falling. The February wind whistled in a thousand languages across the plain darkened by winter and war. It is February in all the infinite lands of the empire, he groaned to himself. Why should he think there might be a fragment of March somewhere, or even a scrap of April? A little March for the empire's chosen sons, he thought. But it was February for everyone.

This was nearly the last of the imperial territories. Two months before, traveling towards this country to take command of the troops after the defeat of Bugrahan, he had noticed that the farther he went from the center and approached the frontier, the minarets were lower, as if they were plants stunted by the increasingly harsh climate. He had been saddened to see those pitiful stumps in the wintry expanse. A little farther, and they no doubt disappeared entirely. There the European plains began, under the sign of the cross. He had never once passed beyond the state borders and had no desire to do so. Some people said that the soil there was saline, and nothing grew but deadly nightshade. Others described it as paradise.

I'm not in my right mind. Why am I doing this, he thought, and shook himself. Why am I doing nothing? He raised his head with a jerk, as if to shake off the sleep creeping over him, and clapped his hands. His adjutants, who stood waiting at a small distance and whom he had not noticed until then, rushed towards him. He motioned his arm as he did before issuing an important order, and began to speak in a voice that to him seemed to come from his temples.

A few moments later, clamorous voices filled Hurshid Pasha's tent. Pashas, battalion commanders, clerics, adjutants, and liaison officers of all kinds ceaselessly came and went, carrying orders, commendations, or reprimands, which they hastened to communicate in exaggerated form to every corner of the vast military camp. Soon the entire besieging army had been informed of the end of the war. News-criers on horseback stopped in front of tents and shouted, "Great news, great news! Ali Pasha has been beheaded. The war is over!"

The whole field buzzed. The wind, which had not died down all day, diminished the human voices, the clatter of horses' hooves, and the clanging of the pots cooking halva for the army, to a dull hum.

At the entrance to Hurshid Pasha's tent, dressed in an official gown with a shaggy cloak thrown over it, appeared the field courier, Tundj Hata. Their eyes met calmly for a moment. The pasha's gaze seemed to say, so you've come? The courier stood there, his face yellow and his beard freshly hennaed, as it usually was before important missions. The henna emphasized even more shockingly the sallowness of his skin.

"So you're ready?" the pasha asked.

"I'm ready," Tundj Hata replied.

Behind his back stood two assistants with bare arms. They held in their hands various strange panniers and pails that no doubt contained the honey and the chunks of ice and salt necessary for the transport and preservation of the head on its long journey.

"Wait outside for my order," said Hurshid Pasha.

The courier bowed. As he went out, their eyes met again. The light of triumph shone in the pasha's eyes. For the past week, Tundj Hata had been wandering about the camp. The very sight of this man, with his awkward limp and muddy face that ended in a short graying beard, had set Hurshid Pasha's stomach churning. But everyone knew that Tundj Hata wouldn't look like this for long; as soon as the order for a head came from the capital, he would collect himself and dye his beard with henna. With the severed head in his pannier, he would leap onto a horse and race through winter and darkness over rough roads or off the highway entirely in order to reach the city as soon as possible. The thought that it could be his own cold head had made Hurshid Pasha shiver, as if he could already feel the handfuls of snow the courier's assistants would carefully pack around it. He had never before been so on edge. He'd lost his temper over everything and nothing. When one of his adjutants had brought him his lunch a few days before, he had thrown the honey-flavored dish in the man's face, screaming, "You dog, who told you I wanted honey? The sight of it makes me sick." And indeed recently he could not bear the sight of honey or salt or ice, and least of all the sight of Tundj Hata, whom he would surely have gotten rid of, if the courier had not been one of those officials who, despite having no particular rank in the state hierarchy, are inviolable and eternal, like the pillars of government buildings.

The pasha sometimes thought that the courier sensed his aversion. He noticed in Tundj Hata's eyes a glint of contained derision, like the play of light at the bottom of a well, as if his eyes were saying, one day I might have your head under my arm, but you'll never have mine. The thought of this truth had nagged at the pasha's mind. More and more often, he remembered a neighbor's cat that, many years ago when he was a boy, had stolen a fish head from the family kitchen as the women shouted and bustled. It seemed to Hurshid Pasha that, in just the same way, Tundj Hata was merely waiting for the moment when, amid the tumult of war, he would seize a head, his own or Ali Pasha's, and gallop with it towards the capital city.

But now all these worries were over. The blade of destiny had harvested its crop, and it was there on the table, this white cabbage from the gardens of hell. The joy that had so far only trickled through in drops now flooded Hurshid

Pasha's entire being. His lethargy vanished. I defeated this old man, he said to himself. I am the one left on this earth.

Voices around him, some faint and others raucous, discussed the best time to set off with the head. Some people said that Tundj Hata should waste no time and leave at once, because the journey was very long. Others shook their beards doubtfully. It would be better to send the head late at night when the world was asleep, to avoid anything unexpected. Two years ago, the couriers transporting the head of the pasha of the sea, Admiral Kara Kiliç, had been attacked. Now in front of them was the head of the empire's most famous vizier and there was every reason for the sultan's enemies to seize it. In fact, Hurshid Pasha's secret wish was that Tundj Hata would lose the head on the road. This was the only chance of the courier losing his own head in turn. But Hurshid Pasha knew that such a thing would never happen. He remembered well the kitchen women striking the thieving cat with their pokers and ladles, but the cat had refused to surrender its trophy. Even if Tundj Hata's hands were cut off, he would carry that head to the Traitor's Niche.

Hurshid Pasha listened to their arguments for a while. He knew that if the head were lost, a government commission would find out why, to the last detail.

"The head will leave at night," he said calmly. "When the world is asleep."

Elation now poured over him in torrents. The storm passed, and infinite rainbows of glory arched above his head.

I have been left alive, he almost cried out loud with a flippant laugh.

He heard the sounds of life around him. Tundj Hata had been summoned to the tent again to be informed of the hour of departure, and his assistants were taking charge of the head. As the pasha's scribe drafted the accompanying report to be handed in to the relevant office, they discussed Tundj Hata's route. Someone pointed out on a map the places where fresh snow could always be found. Somebody suggested "honey from Morea." Someone else noted that in this wintry weather there would be no need to change the ice at all. Then someone asked, "What about the body?"

Everybody turned around in surprise. After an initial bewilderment, the question gradually took shape in their minds. Indeed, what would they do with the body? Hmm, Hurshid Pasha said to himself. Until then, Ali Pasha had been nothing but a head to him. He had totally forgotten the menial body that had carried this head for eighty years.

"The body," Hurshid Pasha said, touching his beard with two fingers. There was something childish in his gesture. "Hmm, the body," he repeated, and smiled, as if to say, amazing, how nature works. But soon he pulled himself together. "Of course we must deal with the body, too," he said. "What do you think?"

They put forward different opinions, but all agreed on the main point that the body must be buried. Unlike their carefully chosen expressions about the head, their language about the body was coarse and plain. They spoke of it with contempt, as if talking about an annoying servant. They soon decided that the body would be buried early in the morning in a simple ceremony on the outskirts of the city, with the honors due to a vizier after his death, albeit a traitorous one.

"And now leave me in peace," Hurshid Pasha said. "I want to rest."

In vain the war correspondents begged him to answer their questions for the newspapers of the capital city.

"Tomorrow," he said. His eyes drooped, as if the laughter that had enlivened them in the last half hour had exhausted them more than all those sleepless nights.

The journalists left, but the pasha, instead of lying down, paced his tent. What a day, he repeated to himself. It was Tuesday. The February wind whistled outside. He saw the pile of newspapers in the corner, his name in black among the headlines, and for a moment he imagined Tuesday as a creature with a trailing black beard ruffled by the wind. Allah, how can you have created days like this? he said to himself.

Two months ago, he had departed from the capital on a day with just such a whistling wind, but before leaving he had entered the cold and lofty halls of the Central Archive to read the file on Ali Pasha. For hours he had studied the correspondence between the sultan and the vizier of Albania. The dates showed the letters becoming less and less frequent. It seemed fitting to read the final ones under the desolate blast of the wind shaking the glass in the high windows of the Archive. "This is my last message to you," the sultan wrote. "If you do not obey me this time, know that you will be consigned to the flames. I will turn you to ash, ash, ash." This was the actual last letter. No reply came from Ali. The couriers had covered the distance between the two continents at incredible speed, their pouches empty. Winter was approaching. The correspondence ceased. After the letters, there would come only ravens and the clouds of war.

I won the war, Hurshid Pasha almost said aloud. I survived. He heard the gale howl again and it seemed to him that he had stumbled and fallen, ensnared by the wind.

The army had gone to bed. The infantry battalions, soldiers and wounded officers, the Anatolian corps, the assault troops, the elderly pashas who suffered from asthma and expected their pensions after this last campaign, and the young pashas, for whom the campaign was the first step in their careers, all lay in rows. Stretched out next to one another were the ensigns, the sheikhs of the death squads, dervishes, spies of the Fourth Directorate, tetanus patients, assistant pronouncers of curses . . . More than half of them were asleep. Their heads rested on the hard pillows, like dying fires in which life sporadically glowed. None of them felt any joy. On the contrary, they were afraid. They had taken part in a huge act of destruction. Their hands had touched the foundations of the state. Deep inside, they sensed that they had tampered with things they should have left alone, and for this they or their offspring could be punished. Their stomachs were heavy with ill-digested halva distributed to mark the victory. Some of them emerged like somnambulists from the tent doors and threw it up, their faces as pale as wax from stomach cramps. The wind still howled from the farthest distances. Beyond this gale there was more wind, and more beyond that.

Even those who slept were not at peace. Some talked in their sleep. Others writhed and thrashed, groaned and fought for breath as they grappled with the void of the night. The wheels of a carriage were heard far away, and someone whispered, "Ali Pasha's head has left." In one of the infantrymen's tents, a soldier moaned in his sleep: "Put the head back on, for God's sake, put the head back on, and stop all this." One of his neighbors whispered to a comrade alongside, "I've heard that in a remote village of Trebizond there's an old barber-surgeon who can fix a severed head. I wrote his name on a bit of paper and stuck it in my army card." His friend listened in silence, and then in horror said, "No, no! That would be too much, if they came back with their heads stuck on, crooked, any old how, in some botched job, and . . ." "What?" asked his friend. But the other soldier had fallen back to sleep. "With heads stuck on crooked," his comrade repeated. Crooked? Why crooked, for God's sake?

The distant sound of wheels reached Hurshid Pasha's ears. He's gone, he thought. Wrapping his shoulders in a woollen blanket, he closed his eyes for the tenth time, but still he couldn't sleep. He felt a constant pressure in his temples. The hissing wind, racing low over the surface of the land, seemed to penetrate his skull. The head has set off for Asia, he thought, but the body remains in Europe. His imagination conjured up some sticky, ectoplasmic creature, pulled by both continents, endlessly lengthening and becoming thinner and more transparent, as if at any moment it might turn into some ethereal substance, something between a cloud and the tail of a comet.

The carriage is heading for Asia, he thought wearily. He is stretching, changing his shape continually, wrapping himself around me. Lying down, Hurshid Pasha felt weak. He propped himself up on his elbow. The thought swept through him, sometimes clearly, sometimes obscurely, that his glory would rise above the other man's ruin. Ali Pasha had been above him for so long, like rolling thunder. Now, under the earth, he would be like some mute crevasse opened by an earthquake. Enough, he said to himself. He has gone. I am still here. It was simple. And indeed for a few moments his mind was clear. But then an old, forgotten phrase came to him from somewhere: "spurned by the grave." So such horrors had been known before.

This thought calmed him a little, and his mind drifted, but then it occurred to him that Ali Pasha would have two graves. Two graves, he repeated to himself. With his entire being, he suddenly yearned for a single grave for himself. He longed for rest, and almost groaned audibly. Wrapping himself again in his woollen blanket, he drowsed for a few moments. He was lying down, at the center of the earth, whole and entire . . . while nearby him were muffled voices. There were plains, with gentle hills, like dough, and apparently a quarrel among them . . . "*grr grr* . . . give me the head . . . you take the body . . . *grr grr* . . ." It was Europe and Asia, quarreling over him . . .

He woke several times during the night. Once his mind remained empty. Another time he asked himself softly, oh God, why aren't things simpler? Towards midnight he started from sleep again. Where am I? he wondered, and then remembered what had happened. I won, he thought drowsily, and huddled deeper in his blanket. It's midnight . . . Tundj Hata was now a black cat with a fish head between his teeth, racing through a landscape of darkness and confusion. Run with that curious fish, Hurshid Pasha thought, and immediately fell asleep.

3

Between the Frontier and the Center of the Empire

MEANWHILE, THE carriage of Tundj Hata the royal courier sped through the bowels of the night. Darkness and nothingness were all around. The plains and the sky had perished, leaving in their place a vast nowhere. Discernible in the gloom was a feeble whiteness, the road, which the carriage followed as if it were a thread that might snap at any moment. From inside his compartment, Tundj Hata could just make out the backs of the two Tatars sitting in front of him. A third was behind him, leaning against the back of the carriage and sheltering it to some extent from the wind. As time passed, Tundj Hata felt that the nothingness and the darkness were severing all his connections to this world. He was overwhelmed by the intoxication he felt on almost every mission of this kind. Amid the death of everything, he felt free. Waves of elation flowed over him, one after another, breaking against the inside of his chest, filling the space of his lungs with foam, and roaring through his swelling veins.

Tundj Hata sensed eyes in the darkness watching him

from all directions through the panes of the carriage windows. He cried out. But neither of the guards in front or behind him moved. The cry was inside himself. Tundj Hata felt that his last links to this world were breaking. His frenzy increased, as if he were being sucked into a whirlpool. He had felt the same way one week before, when making this journey in the opposite direction, from the capital to the frontier, with two decrees bound to his body, one hidden under his right arm, one under his left. Both decrees bore the wax of the royal seal and carried the sultan's signature, but one had been false. The genuine one was the death sentence, or *katil ferman*, as it was known in the archaic jargon of officialdom. On that journey, Tundj Hata had sensed that one of the wax-sealed letters his chest was warming would soon be turned into a head. The transformation took place within a week. The letter had brought death, and he had been its messenger.

Tundj Hata gave a second cry. But still the guards heard nothing. Now he hovered in a void entirely alone, as if catapulted into the outer universe. He was far away in the depths of a black space that nobody had ever penetrated. He was its master, and at the same time its slave. He felt himself swell and bristle and simultaneously shrink and melt. He gave a third cry and at once, with a jerk, he hunched his body over the severed head that he was holding by his side. His face touched its cold curls. He drew his lips close to the ear and whispered, "Now we're on our way. Can you hear the wheels on the gravel? We're off, we're off." For a long time he muttered disconnected words into the head's icy ear. "Hahaha" or "hehehe," he went, but thought he was saying more or less this: You are, or rather were, the great Ali Pasha and when you were him, you never knew that a certain Tundj Hata lived in this world. You would have split your sides with laughter, hahaha, hehehe, if anyone had told you that one day Tundj Hata the courier would have any business with you. Hahaha, you would have gone, hehehe, you would have put your hands on your hips in gales of laughter until you were out of breath, and the servants would have come running with glasses of water, calling the chief steward, the doctor, the physician-in-chief. Hahaha, hehehe . . . But look now how night has come and I have your head under my arm. It's my turn to go hahaha, hehehe. Me and the February wind. Hahaha, hoohoohoo. One winter night like this, years ago, on a tedious tour of duty, my journey took me along the main road near your capital city. It was cold and I was miserable. From my carriage, I glimpsed the lights of your palace in the distance. They were far away, like stars. I did not take my eyes off them for a long time. Pasha, you have risen to a great height, I thought, wrapping my courier's fleece more tightly around me. And at that moment I felt a kind of dizziness. My entire body cried, you will be mine. Mine, and here you are, hahaha, hehehe. I waited for so many years, like waiting for a fruit tree to mature. Other fruit fell, and I carefully carried them—here, under this arm—while your branches grew higher and higher. But I knew that your own time would come. Your own time, hahaha, hehehe. You lofty state grandees pass by us middling officials, unreach-able, with contempt in your half-closed eyes, not deigning even to turn your heads. At state dinners you sit at the top tables in your fine clothes, with your glittering medals, hold-ing your necks straight as only you know how. Whereas we, the middling sort, barely squeeze around the lowest table, near the guards and servers. We watch you from a distance. We watch you, hahaha, hehehe. We wait for you to fall, we wait to carry you like this under our arms, taking you far, far away. Faster, coachman, hahaha . . .

Tundj Hata went on murmuring into the head's ear for some time, but eventually grew tired. His exaltation sub-sided. He felt cold, wrapped himself more tightly in his sheepskin, and rested his head against the back of the seat. He was exhausted, as if by some epileptic fit. He felt a pres-sure on his temples and a bitter taste in his mouth. This always happened after the first storm passed. Drained and empty, he huddled in a corner of the carriage hoping for a lit-tle sleep. But after such agitation, no sleep would come. The higher his rank, the more he craved sleep. The excitement was more powerful to him than the lure of women, and the higher the rank of the head, the more thrilling the sensation was. Now drained, he recalled his first journey with a head, like a famous drunkard telling the story of his first binge to the village inn.

It had been summer. The weather was sultry and stifling. There was no snow to be found anywhere. He stopped now and then to refresh the severed head at cold springs. He was inexperienced. He had been working for one year as a courier for the court's Third Branch and had carried decrees and orders of all kinds, but never a head. And as if this were not difficult enough, it was the height of summer. At any moment, the head could spoil. As he traveled, he opened the pannier and looked in anxiously. Allah, he said to himself, what have we mortals done to be put to this test, traveling with heads in our hands? A huge moon drowned the world in its light. Now and then he opened *Regulations for the Care of Heads of the Condemned* and under the light of the moon read and reread the chapter "On the Use of Salt." The head sat next to him, a handsome head with strangely calm eyes. The grains of salt on its hair, eyebrows, and cheeks glittered under the moon. For a moment, he lifted his eyes from the rulebook and sat entranced by the sight. Without realizing it, he had drawn close to the ear and for the first time whispered, "My bride." More words followed, first dripping like sweat, sometimes cold, sometimes warm, then in an indistinguishable torrent of rage and love.

That had been his first taste of this intoxication. It recurred on his later missions, until it became something he could not live without.

Tomorrow, Tundj Hata said to himself, and his mind wandered, thinking of the route they would take the next day. His imagination raced in front of the carriage, faster than the horses, sliding like the shadow of a cloud over the broad wastelands and wretched villages that looked as if they were perpetually waiting for something. The wheels creaked plaintively and Tundj Hata recalled the night he carried the governor of Tripoli's head. It had been winter, with gales and fog. The carriage had hit a roadside post and all its windows had shattered. The sleet had soaked Tundj Hata to the bone. He tried to protect the pannier that conveyed the governor's head, but it was impossible. During the flashes of lightning, the severed head with its drenched and disheveled hair looked somehow indignant. Tundj Hata, against his custom and against all instructions (couriers transporting heads were forbidden to stop on the way), was forced to take shelter in the first inn he came across. It was one of those hundreds of ordinary inns on the great highway, and only its name was particular, the Inn of the Two Roberts. On other kinds of missions, he had often spent the night in such refuges. Almost without exception, they consisted of a room with a fire, around whose hearth the guests sat after dinner, especially in winter. In most cases the travelers were officials of different ranks on state business. It was not difficult to distinguish the dignitaries of the capital city, on tours of superior inspection, from the provincial officials who'd been summoned to the capital. Around the wintry fire, guests who were strangers would at first be cautious with one another. But after the initial frostiness, both sides usually talked until late: senior officials liked to impress their audience with stories from the capital, and the provincials were pleased to be included in the conversation at all. Their talk ranged over all kinds of topics, from the recent high-level appointments and dismissals, a subject dear to the hearts of all civil servants, to the private lives of famous people in the arts. Tundj Hata generally sat apart. Although he had never carried an artist's head in his official bag, to him the fame of artists was just as ephemeral as the splendor of the great offices of state.

On that stormy night, sodden and with his leather pannier in hand, Tundj Hata arrived at the inn in a fury. The terrified innkeeper was unable to judge who this man was or where he had come from. But Tundj Hata couldn't have cared less. He barged into the main room, where seven or eight guests were stretched out beside the hearth. Almost all of them turned towards the new arrival, ready to welcome him, as one would receive any person coming in from a storm. But Tundj Hata's face was so wild that it repelled not only their sympathy but questions of any kind. Heedless of them all and without a greeting, he approached the fire and roughly took his place, shouldering in between two guests. Everybody's expressions changed from surprise to concern, and then under a strenuous silence this stranger thrust his hands in his pannier and drew out by the hair a severed head. Before the startled eyes of the guests, he positioned the drenched head beside the fire, supposedly to dry it.

Tundj Hata did not even want to know who these guests were whom he had treated with such contempt. He realized later that, with the exception of a villager traveling to the capital for the removal of a stomach ulcer and two hashish merchants on their way to Province Six, the other guests were civil servants: two senior clerics on their way to inspect the dervish lodges in the European region of the state, a diplomatic courier, and an important official who some thought was the deputy director of a bank and others an employee of the Interior Ministry. All these people exchanged glances several times with wide-open eyes and then sat nonplussed, not knowing which of their number should be the first person, by rank, to explode in fury at this newcomer. Finally, almost in unison, the hoarse voices of the two clerics and the deputy bank director or secret police official were heard, and then joined by all the other guests and the innkeeper himself, who approached gripping a stave. Tundj Hata stared at them first with contempt and then loathing. Their voices turned to shouts, and out of the corner of his eye Tundj Hata saw the innkeeper raise the stave threateningly. The courier straightened his back and with a sudden flourish produced the official travel order with the imperial seal. On this was written in black on white that he, Tundj Sar Aksham Hata, courier of the court's Third Branch, was charged with the duty of carrying to the capital the severed head of the governor of Tripoli, demanded by writ of the sultan on the seventh of December. This letter brandished in front of their faces had a sedative effect, silencing their cries and magically transforming the innkeeper's stave into a harmless piece of wood. Tundj Hata had no desire to crow over his victory. Wearily he returned the letter to his breast pocket (the crackling of the thick paper was audible in the silence) and, without a glance at his fellow guests, passed his hands two or three times through the still-icy hair of the head almost tenderly, not taking his eyes off it, as if to say: They don't care for you. What have you done to them, I wonder, to turn them against you?

Silence fell around the hearth, and the flames and embers were the only life. The hair of the head began to steam in the warmth. The vapor rose like a mist straight from the kingdom of death. Behind this haze, the eyes of the guests were dull and glazed, yet with a strange glint, as if this steam were sulfurous incense sending them into a state of religious ecstasy. They sat late into the night. As he watched their eyes fade, Tundj Hata thought vaguely of the line of people outside the doors of the royal theater. He did not then understand that this association of images was not accidental. In his mind, if dimly, the idea had been born that a severed head could fascinate an audience just as much as a work of art. He thought of the queues for opening-night tickets and their high prices. And for the first time, there by the hearth in that inn with its filthy name, the idea struck him that . . . in the course of his journey . . . somewhere . . . in remote villages . . . where there had never been a theater . . . he, and the severed head . . . (queue for tickets, queue for tickets, queue for tickets). It was perhaps midnight or later when he abruptly roused himself, drew a handful of white salt out of his bag, and sprinkled it on the severed head (rather like an actor putting on makeup before a performance). With an unexpected "good night" to everybody he put the head back in the pannier and departed with it for his own room. Tomorrow, tomorrow, he repeated to himself as he climbed the rickety stairway.

A long time had passed since that night. Tundj Hata's

memory went back again and again to that roadside inn, distorting the shape of the stairs, the windows, and the wooden sign by the gate with the inscription "Inn of the Two Roberts," rendering indistinct the faces of the guests, and retaining only one thing unaltered: those stupefied eyes staring through the vapor that rose from the locks of dead hair.

Now the head of Ali Pasha, who had been a vizier of this world where the February wind blew, was here beside him, and far ahead lay villages without theaters but with plenty of eager eyes. Tomorrow, he said to himself again. You will see it tomorrow, he said for the third time, and tried to encourage sleep to occupy at least a part of his mind. But his riotous thoughts would not obey him. As soon as he suppressed some, others rebelled. This went on through the night until, just after the second change of horses at a post station, his fit came again.

Towards dawn, the carriage still trundled on with the same monotonous sound. The darkness was now less dense and reminded Tundj Hata of a horse stripped of its hair. Day felt closer. Like every new regime, the daylight would turn everything upside down, bring down mountains of shadows and raise new mountains, change the dimensions of things, destroy entire prospects and impose its own signs and symbols everywhere. Only the wind, ready to serve the day as much as the night, remained unaffected in its howling indifference, whatever its direction.

Tundj Hata felt himself become heavier and more squat as day approached. His limbs, which during the elation of the night had grown infinitely longer, had suddenly contracted, his mind was sluggish, and his eyesight weak. On the verge of sleep, he brought his face up to the windowpane in a final effort to find out where he was. In front of him was a river swollen by winter, which looked to him like the Ujana e Keqe. It was indeed this river, with the famous three-arched bridge over it. This meant that the Albanian lands would soon come to an end.

The carriage wheels struck the paving on the hump of the bridge, and Tundj Hata trembled, shaken less by the sudden shock to the carriage than by the thought of passing over this cursed structure. This bridge was ancient, almost five hundred years old, and there was a legend about it that made your flesh creep, like all Balkan tales. It was said that they had immured a person in one of the three arches.

Tundj Hata could not tear his eyes away from the swirling water. On his several journeys by this route, he had heard scraps of the ballad: for a long time the spirit of the water had not allowed a bridge to be built over the river (everything that the masons built during the day was destroyed at night), until the builders realized that the water was demanding a sacrifice.

What a repulsive fiction, he said to himself. What was the Central Archive doing, allowing such legends to survive? It was one of the few things in the course of his life that had terrified him. He had written an anonymous letter to the

Sheikh-ul-Islam, accusing the Central Archive of dereliction of its duty. But still the legend lived on.

The crossing of the bridge seemed to Tundj Hata horribly prolonged. One arch after another loomed into view. The centuries had darkened the stone of the bridge and encrusted its piers with green moss. The bridge had grown old, and the immured victim had been impossible to discern since long ago. The wind had eroded his features and nobody could tell where his face and neck had been. Anyone ignorant would not have been able to detect the outlines of a human form under this petrified crust.

Ugh, thought Tundj Hata, trying to wrench his eyes away from the final arch. At the end of the bridge on the right-hand side was a mausoleum, as old as the bridge itself. It had been built in memory of the first bloody encounter between Ottoman and Albanian troops, which had happened on this very bridge over the Ujana e Keqe. The inscription at the entrance to the mausoleum explained everything: the date of the incident and its consequences, and the name of the Turkish soldier who was killed, one Ibrahim, whose blood was the first drop of the great rivers of Ottoman blood that were to be shed over this land.

Ugh, went Tundj Hata for a second time, as he felt the carriage wheels leave the bridge behind. He leaned into the back of his seat, and only when it was fully daylight did he breathe on the windowpane to see where he was. We must be out of Albania, he thought. He looked abstractedly at the frost-covered earth. It was hard to find anything else in the world that was so ordinary yet so widespread. At least let snow cover the earth, he said to himself, and why wasn't snow black, like the veils of women? After all, the soil is nothing but a fertile woman. An old whore. That was why high officials went even crazier for land than for women.

The old whore, Tundj Hata almost said aloud, staring at the frost that lay like white powder over the sleepy surface of the field. He felt exhausted. The thought slid snail-like through his mind that his second fit, towards dawn, had worn him out completely. It had been too much, he said to himself. It was like mounting a woman in the morning. Now he felt that his mind not only lacked the strength to forge ahead, but was trapped in his skull and unable to rise to the simplest thought. Tundj Hata was benumbed, seized by a frightening insensibility. At these moments, his face looked more terrifying than it did during his most savage agitation, as when he took part in mass executions or flirted with severed heads. He stared at the wintry landscape, or rather it passed icily into his field of vision. Small muddy towns, villages that from a distance looked embalmed, churches, tall minarets, the yellow house of an estate owner, a leper colony, lime pits, bridges, a town under quarantine because of the plague, bare poplars, roadside inns—all these lurched past, close or distant, boiled together as if in some thick glue. For him this entire world was something mummified. At one point, near a crossroads, he saw a wedding party with the bride veiled and on horseback. His imagination wandered between her legs, to her genitals irritated by the saddle, and he chuckled. In fact he merely thought he chuckled . . . nothing in his expression moved. His laughter, like some tiny beetle deep underground, would have miles to burrow before emerging at the surface.

Tundj Hata shook off his apathy to some degree at the third change of horses, where he had to buy snow for the head. He had hoped to find snow on the hillsides along the road, but there was only a thin slush, impossible to gather. Real snow, like some great lady in white, looked down disdainfully from hundreds of yards farther up. He haggled with the peasant over the price, and called him a leech for sucking a man's blood for a handful of snow that he might collect himself if he had time. But the man told him that the weather was warm, and that he'd soon be begging for even a little hoarfrost. Then Tundj Hata would pay for a handful of snow with its weight in silver. "It's not summer yet . . ." Tundj Hata retorted. Summer seemed a long way off, and he believed it would never come.

He repacked the head before the peasant's astonished gaze. It looked like one of the snowmen that children build in the winter holidays. He took care when covering the most delicate parts of the face, especially the eyes.

The carriage moved off again, followed by the derisive stare of the peasant, who seemed to be saying, see you in the summer, Mr. Courier. From the rear window of the carriage, Tundj Hata watched the peasant as he emptied the remaining snow on the ground and stamped on it, as if scared that someone else might use it.

Above the gray plateau stretched a sky as broad as the land itself, with a bald red sun, shorn of its surrounding rays.

They had left Albania behind a long time ago and were approaching the territories that had been stripped of their nationality: Provinces Two, Six, and Seven. Together these formed the broad region under Caw-caw, usually marked in pale pink on the maps of the empire.

Tundj Hata, totally stupefied, pressed his head against the carriage window to look; his temples felt the shaking of the glass.

This is how he always remembered the endless plateau of the Caw-caw region, with a perpetually cold sun that was dull red like sealing wax, as if the sovereign had decreed that its days should look like this.

The featureless road stretched endlessly ahead. Here even the milestones had no figures. Numbers must have been erased along with letters when these parts were stripped of their language.

Whenever he took this route, Tundj Hata did all he could to pass the time sleeping but, amazingly, it was precisely here, in the empire's most somnolent region, that sleep eluded him. He stared at the monotonous road, waiting for the approach of the next milestone. It would gleam in the distance, a mere dot, and then quickly grow larger until it passed the carriage, rinsed by the rains and bleached by the sun, with no number or other marking. Then Tundj Hata would heave an involuntary sigh and wait for the next stone.

He was shaken out of this daze when, shortly before noon,

the first village deputation stepped out in front of the carriage. The four men had been sitting by the roadside, cowering against the cold, bundled up in sleeveless and collarless tunics like gray felt sacks, such as all the inhabitants of the degraded territories were forced to wear. They told the Tatars that they had seen the carriage in the distance from their village, which was barely visible on a mountain spur, and had hurried down the slope to meet them.

When Tundj Hata opened the door painted with the royal arms, the four bowed almost to the ground.

"There is a head," said Tundj Hata loftily, not even glancing down. He looked to one side in a direction where there was nothing to be seen. They bowed even lower, perhaps to the dead man as well. But Tundj Hata did not even get out of his carriage. He knew that the words *there is a head* had a magical effect. When there was no head, Tundj Hata himself would smile at them, as if begging pardon. He would inquire about their health and their crops, assure them that next time he would come bearing something, and even produce from his chest his travel order, passing it around. They would stare in silence at the yellow seals, which enclosed death, and tell him they would look out for him again. But now that there was a head, Tundj Hata sat in lofty silence, as if to create the impression he had cut this head especially for them. They waited in vain for him to ask them about their flocks and their ailments. He knew that any chatter of this kind would devalue the show. Still he sat in the carriage, staring to one side. Finally, he announced in a metallic voice, giving every word equal weight:

"The head of Ali Tepelena, governor of Albania, a pasha of the highest rank, a member of the Council of Ministers."

They froze on the spot. Their felt jackets barely contained their shaking shoulders. They glanced at one another, and then tried to catch the courier's eye. But they could not.

"Well," Tundj Hata said at last. "How much will you give?"

Two or three opened their mouths to speak, but only one managed to shape a few words.

"Mr. Courier . . . this year we . . . this year . . . one disaster after another . . . Mr. Courier . . . this year . . . because . . . you see why . . ."

"What?" Tundj Hata howled. "Are you trying to tell me you want to see heads more cheaply? Are heads not worth a decent price?"

Two peasants bowed to kiss the running board where the courier would place his foot. But Tundj Hata did not get out.

"Speak up!" he said from above, but to himself he cursed them. "You think these heads are easy to find, like cuts from some slaughterhouse? You don't deserve one. Not this one, which is a head surpassing all others, nor even the head of some mean scribe who made a mistake copying a document. You don't deserve the head of a banker or a curse-giver. All you deserve is the head of some thief or sodomite or adulterous wife. The sort you find in prison yards. That's all you deserve."

They were now visibly shaking. Finally one of them showed the palm of his hand, on which lay some pebbles. Tundj Hata studied them. The peasants did not know numbers, and this was the only way they could tell him what price they offered.

"Seven sovereign," said Tundj Hata, raising his eyebrows in surprise. "For the four of you," he added . . . "What?" he exclaimed angrily. "For the whole village?" His hennaed beard looked as if it would catch fire in the wind. "Seven pounds to see the head of Ali Pasha, the great sultan's rival? You must be crazy."

Terrified that he would stalk away, the four set aside their caution and began chattering among themselves, clumsily interrupting one another with as much vigor as their halting patois permitted. They said that Mr. Courier should try to show a little understanding, that this winter had been truly disastrous for them, that anthrax had attacked their livestock, wolves had eaten two shepherds, their baker had come back as a vampire three days after his death, and if all this were not enough (here they lowered their voices) it was said that the priest's middle daughter was pregnant, and a horrible thing had happened to the old woman Xune, the like of which nobody in the village and perhaps the entire district could remember: she had received a letter in the post. Surely this letter had been sent by the devil himself, so the whole village had assembled, led by their imam, to spit on it and burn it and scatter its ashes into the air. The more they rambled on with their trivia, the more Tundj Hata was convinced they were in thrall to his showmanship. He couldn't remember which head he had shown them last time, but it must have been an exceptionally alluring one, to dazzle them to this extent. It would be hard to find such dedicated spectators even at the entrance to the royal circus in the capital city, even when the famous Tor Djanaydini was performing.

They had now raised their offer, but Tundj Hata had already decided what he would do. Without casting them a glance, he slammed the carriage door shut before their very noses. The wretched creatures ran after the carriage wheels, shouting, "Wait! Wait!" but Tundj Hata did not even turn his head. He knew that next time they would pay triple the price without a whimper, to see some quite insignificant head.

That afternoon, Tundj Hata came across the next deputation, which, seen through the window clouded with the courier's breath, resembled a bunch of rags flapping in the wind. When Tundj Hata called out, "I have a head," the people fell to the ground. A price was hurriedly agreed. Tundj Hata told them that his time was precious and they set off towards the village on a puddle-strewn, potholed road. Some of the people pushed the carriage forward and tried to kiss the wheels.

The village stood between a ravine and a stretch of burned woodland, its huts and hovels so tightly packed in the midst of the endless plain as to resemble a flock of sheep huddled in fear.

Panting, the deputation told how they had been watching the road all week, and just when they were losing hope, the carriage appeared and they had hurried to intercept it.

Tundj Hata listened to their tale with indifference. This person who was so unaffected by their story, which they had racked their brains all week to devise, must really be an important gentleman.

The streets were totally deserted as they entered the village. The population had gathered under the porch of the mosque. This was a large, extremely cold portico, and the people stood motionless in expectation, without a whisper. Tundj Hata climbed the steps to the mosque, taking the leather bag from the Tatar who was carrying it and leading the way under the porch. His assistants followed him and they took their places behind a wooden bench in front of the crowd. Tundj Hata looked at the unmoving heads of men, women, old people, and children, and it struck him that they looked so frozen that if they had to be transported they wouldn't need snow or salt or even *Regulations for the Care of Heads*, which all the couriers carried with their travel papers.

Tundj Hata laid the bag on the wooden bench and announced in a resounding voice:

"Ali Tepelena, Black Ali, governor of Albania, a pasha of the first rank, and member of the Council of Ministers."

As he uttered the last word, he put his hand in the bag and, gripping the head by the hair, drew it out in a swift movement. It resembled less a head than a packed chunk of snow, through which strands of grizzled hair were intermittently visible. Tundj Hata began to pick off the snow. First he exposed the right eye, and then the nose, the cheeks, the other eye, the eyebrows, and the full face, a wan gray.

The silence, already total, deepened, as if within this silence a gate to some abyss had opened.

The head was establishing its rapport with the crowd. Its glassy eyes sought human eyes. Death hung in the air, transparently visible. As the cold tightened its grip, the spectators felt drawn closer to the frontier of death, almost touching it. In a few moments the crowd and death would congeal in a waxen, translucent unity.

This happened at all the shows. Tundj Hata knew that for remote, buried hamlets, this spectacle was at the same time their literature, theater, art, philosophy, and perhaps love. (He could not forget the shout of "Oh, how young he is!" from a girl, as he was wiping the snow from the head of the "blond pasha." It was the only human voice he had ever heard during a showing.)

Tundj Hata looked at the drawings on the walls of the mosque, behind which the choirs of Christian saints, roughly effaced, could still be discerned. The building itself, if you looked at it carefully, preserved the shape of a church. It had swallowed the old chapel without digesting it. He had noticed that churches that were turned into mosques came back as soon as they could in a shadowy form, like the shape he had once seen of a woman drowned in a pond, which emerged as the water cleared.

During these shows, Tundj Hata had noticed that as much

as he tried to turn his thoughts back to practical things, such as the money he might earn by the end of the journey, he could not escape the intimation of death. The most universal, immaterial things passed through his mind. Perhaps this was the very reason these lost souls gave him money, to stir up their thoughts for a few moments. It was as if their minds, like fat chickens, could not take flight without being startled by something, in this case by death.

Tundj Hata thought they had seen enough. He reached out to the chunks of snow that surrounded the head like a torn collar of white fur, and this gesture instantly broke that fragile intersection of life and death, more delicate than anything else in this world. Tundj Hata's hands deftly separated death from life again as he covered the head with snow. First one eye vanished, then the cheeks, then the other eye, and soon the head was turned back into an icy lump. Grasping it with both hands, he put it in the bag, and at the same moment the crowd filling the mosque porch moved, as if released from some hook that had kept them suspended above an abyss. Tundj Hata took the money and hurried away. At the carriage, he gave half a sovereign to each of the three Tatars. They leaped into their seats and the vehicle set off. Tundj Hata stared at the milestones, some upright, some tilting where the soil had slid or a cart had struck them.

After the third show, Tundj Hata looked thoughtfully at the sky. Dusk was falling and a fourth show was unlikely. Not because of the light—on the contrary, in the evening, a display by torchlight could have twice the impact—but because there wasn't enough time. They were already hurrying to make up the lost hours, but they could only go so fast. If he were late for no reason, a file might be opened to investigate him, and that would be his end.

As the Tatars urged on the horses, Tundj Hata looked back at the village for the last time. It lay huddled and cowed in the open plain, with a long and troubled night ahead of it.

Fine rain began to fall. The milestones grew fainter, and soon they would have to light the lanterns. The previous night they had traveled without them, because the sky, although moonless and starless, had been suffused with a kind of vestigial glow. But tonight the sky was unyielding.

Night had long fallen when they encountered the last deputation. The peasants emerged from the darkness like large beetles. One of them held a torch, which he raised and lowered to help him see. From inside the carriage, Tundj Hata watched the patches of jaundiced light that flickered from the puddles on the road to the carriage wheels and the backs of the Tatars. He heard scattered voices, muffled and terrified, and shouts of "Is there a head?" The rattling carriage plowed through them without stopping, as if through a nightmare.

After this they met nobody. The earth and sky stretched ahead, indifferent in their immensity. Tundj Hata felt the night was attempting to envelop the whole empire. But it couldn't. The empire was larger than the night. People said that when dusk fell at one end, dawn rose at the other. The blanket of night was not large enough to cover the whole body of the state. Either its head or its feet would be left outside. The head or the feet, he thought, and unconsciously felt for the sack with his hand. If the head were Albania, the feet would be near the border of Hindustan, or the other way around. No, he thought. The empire resembled least of all a human body. Like most states, it had its head in the center. Listlessly, he tried to call to mind some creature with its head in the middle of its body, but could not do so. Beasts such as the lion or dragon, whose images appeared on many state emblems and seals, all had their heads at one end of their body. Aha, he almost exclaimed aloud. There was one creature with its head in the middle, the octopus. He hurriedly pictured in his mind all the gates to government buildings he had ever passed through but could not remember a single one carved or painted with the emblem of an octopus. Scared that he might have entertained a sinful thought, he banished the image from his own head, which at once, as if freed from a final burden, sank forward between his shoulders.

He dozed for a short time. But then he was jolted as if slapped by an invisible hand. He pressed his forehead to the window and stared out into the darkness. He could tell that it was coming. As always, when the exaltation approached, his breath quickened. Then his entire being surged forward, straining to race ahead of the carriage, the horses, the Tatars, and even his own body with its sheath of skin, its eyes, ears, and its weight. His physical body fell behind him, as if drowning in chaos. He felt he was shedding it forever. He leaned to the right and his temples touched the icy locks of the head. He recoiled from the touch and the first involuntary gulps escaped him: "Huhuhu, hahaha." Then everything repeated itself as on the previous night. His brain resembled some clinging creature with the inner luminescence of a glowworm, whose slime smeared the domes of mosques and mausoleums, banknotes, and the wombs of women awaiting insemination.

After the first attack, the intoxication came back to him twice more, before and after midnight. Totally crushed, he detached himself at last from the severed head with a painful groan. "We're getting close," he whispered to it. "Can you tell we're getting close?"

During lucid moments when he was capable of thought, he recalled the square in the capital city where the "stone of deterrence" stood. The niche was currently vacant and he almost cried aloud: The square's empty, waiting for us. We must hurry.

A thousand times he asked himself, what is the point of that square without a head? What wakes up the square in the mornings, and how does it pass the afternoons? And he urged the Tatars to drive faster, as if they were hurrying to reach a person who would give up the ghost if they were even slightly late.

The darkness was thinning, and here and there the sleeping land was visible behind a scant veil of mist. It sprawled out, with its provocative undulations bursting with desire, and who knows how this shameless whore would sport herself in freedom, if the imperial capital were not on the far horizon, like some lion crouching on its front paws, snarling and spreading fear throughout the world.

What would the world be like without this city? The thought was so monstrous and terrifying that he instantly wondered if such a thing were possible. God forbid, he almost cried aloud, and shook his head.

The capital was drawing closer. There was no sign to indicate it, no arrow pointing towards it, no chimney smoke, but its chill presence could be felt. Everything around it was shrouded in a solemn silence. The city is still asleep, Tundj Hata thought. His teeth chattered.

There! He did not know what it was he saw: the tip of some tower, the point of a minaret, or perhaps a bird gliding in that motionless flight peculiar to birds hovering above domes. He straightened his back in fear. His limbs, loose and yielding after his nighttime ecstasy, snapped back into their usual positions. He felt weight returning to his body, his veins knitting his reluctant members together, as if binding them in fetters, shrinking and compressing them into human shape.

Finally the towers of the capital appeared on the cold horizon. Distant, frigid in eternal drabness, they loomed one after another, according to their hierarchy of height: the leaden dome of the Temple of the Ottoman Spirit, the pinnacles of the minarets of Hagia Sophia, the Obelisk of Tokmakhan, the Central State Archive, the Sublime Porte, the pillars of the Imperial Bank, the pale blue domes of the Palace of Dreams, the centuries-old Palace of Psst-Psst and the Palace of Seals and Decrees. There was the flag above the War Ministry. They all seemed to be waiting for him.

Tundj Hata could not tear his eyes from the vision into which the carriage was now sucking him, as if into a dream.

The sentries of the Seventh Gate saw the carriage from a distance. One of them raised a spyglass to his eye.

"The imperial courier," he said, keeping the spyglass clamped to his right eye.

The other two guards also watched the black rectangle gradually grow in size, imagining the state emblem on its doors and box, which their colleague could now clearly discern through the lens.

It was still early. The barren plain surrounding the capital was blotched with mist. The guard watched the moving coach. In the semidarkness, it might have struck an observer that he was not holding a spyglass but trying in vain to remove an iron bar that had been driven into his eye. With awkward steps the other two descended the stone stairway to open the gate. A squeal of iron was heard, and then the carriage wheels, very close. The guard removed the spyglass from his eye and leaned over the stone parapet to see the new arrival, who descended from the carriage and showed the other sentries his travel papers. The guard rested his chin on his fist and studied the movements of the small group. When the new arrival suddenly raised his head, the guard shivered. He had never seen a more repulsive face. Below a scarred brow, the eyes seemed stuck on from outside. A red triangular beard contrasted with the yellow wax of his skin.

The guard reluctantly turned his eyes away to the inscrutable wasteland whose February mist had spawned this creature.

After the carriage wheels had rattled through the gate, the other sentries rejoined him above.

"The head of Ali Pasha of Albania," said one.

The guard with the spyglass jerked around. "Impossible," he said.

"We saw it with our own eyes, it was in the leather pannier, with the ears poking out of the ice."

"It can't be," the first guard insisted.

"You never believe anything."

The guard with the spyglass kept his eyes fixed on the road. Really, there was nothing not to believe. The sentries of the Seventh Gate were always the first to learn of the arrival of a governor's head from the empire's European territories. Heads from Asian provinces entered the capital by the First Gate.

Of course, he said to himself, instantly forgetting why it should be so obvious. Of course, he remembered again. This man's head was bound to arrive at this gate one morning. As everybody knew, diplomatic bags, important delegations, and the heads of executed men entered the capital through only the Seventh and First Gates. This had been established by a special decree and there could be no confusion. No confusion, he repeated to himself. There was no way messengers with state correspondence or heads could pass through the Second or Fourth Gates, which were used for meat and vegetables and other supplies for the capital, and by foreign tourists. There were regulations and even precise schedules for all these things, in order to avoid congestion. The Seventh and First Gates were both opened very seldom. Indeed, they were not opened at all for days on end, and during heavy frost, as in the previous month, their hinges and bolts froze and hot water had to be thrown at them before they would move. Of course, he said to himself for the third time. It wasn't the same as bringing cabbages. Yet in a way, he thought as he looked out at the infinite wilderness, barely visible in the February light, these heads resembled large vegetables.

The sound of the carriage had faded some time ago. Now the head must be nearing the center, he thought, and turned around to face the city. Its tall towers and the bronze and leaden needles of the minarets shone with an inner light. The head has arrived, the guard said to himself. The capital city had been waiting for that little bundle packed in snow and salt for a long time. The other gates stuffed the city with meat, cheese, and vegetables, but still couldn't satisfy its hunger. More than anything, it needed to have that head.

4

The Center of the Empire.
Cloudy Day

ALI TEPELENA's head had been placed in the Traitor's
Niche two hours ago. Abdulla, looking pale in a new
dark suit cut for his wedding day, stood in his usual place
with his hands behind him, looking at the crowds milling
about the square. Bugrahan Pasha's head had been removed
five days before, and the niche had remained empty. Without
a head on display, the square seemed perplexed, confused,
distracted. The crowds wandered blindly, and scattered in all
directions. The square lost its focus. Now that it had a head
again, everything fell back into place. The square recovered
its usual bustle. The streams of people flowed with a regular-
ity that reminded Abdulla of the tides of the sea drawn by
the moon. The head placed on the side of the square exerted
a pull like some heavenly entity.

Even when the square had been without a head, Abdulla's
rules of service had required him to remain in his place. This
was for two reasons. First and foremost, although the niche
might be empty, people should not have the impression that

punishments had stopped, and Abdulla's presence in his usual position suggested that a severed head might appear in the niche at any moment. The second reason was simple: Abdulla had to keep an eye on the niche to prevent anyone defiling it, whether as a provocation against the state or simply in an act of madness. Two years ago, some unidentified delinquents had left a frozen skylark on its ledge.

During those days when the niche had been empty, one could discern a question in the eyes of the people passing by. Whose head would be next—Ali Pasha's or Hurshid Pasha's? A similar question had been asked before: Ali Pasha's or Bugrahan Pasha's? Most people expected Hurshid to follow the fate of Bugrahan, and no doubt bets had been made in secret. However, the reverse turned out to be true, and Ali the victorious was now vanquished.

His head had arrived in the capital city in total secrecy more than twenty-four hours ago, before dawn, but the news had spread in whispers an hour before the official proclamation. Crowds hurried to the square in the hope of seeing the head of the most powerful man in the empire, after the sultan, but all day the niche had remained empty. Questions came thick and fast—what was going on? why weren't they bringing it? when would they? what?—and it seemed to Abdulla that such speculation had filled the square since the beginning of time. He knew that there was every reason for the delay in bringing the head. At ten o'clock, after receiving the customary cosmetic attention, it had been presented to the sultan-emperor. Nobody yet knew for certain how long the silver dish had remained in front of the sultan, what the ruler had said, and whether he had expressed any general opinion on the subject of separatism. All that was known was that at eleven o'clock the head was presented to the most senior state and religious dignitaries in the building of the Council of State. At half past twelve, foreign ambassadors were summoned to view the head, and at one o'clock the grand vizier announced at a short press conference that in spite of the uprising of the province of the Albanians, the empire's unity was now stronger than ever. However, he announced, the government would continue to punish with the greatest severity any separatist tendencies displayed by anybody in whatever corner of the realm.

Clearly, the grand vizier's speech threatened every region of the mighty state, especially those provinces that enjoyed a degree of autonomy, as Albania had done until recently. In severe tones, the grand vizier stressed that the Sublime Porte would henceforth not permit any misinterpretation of this autonomy, and still less its abuse. Foreign observers were particularly struck by the part of the speech in which the vizier, in the name of the government and the sultan-emperor, laid down a new definition of the autonomy of the provinces. For years, the official press had glorified the benefits of this autonomy as the clearest expression of the flourishing state of the peoples of the imperial family. On this point, the vizier said that even though the great Ottoman state consisted of nationalities with different names, in fact these peoples, before they were Turks, Albanians, Greeks, Serbs, Bosnians,

Tatars, Caucasians, and so on, were members of a common Islamic nation. History provided many examples of the fate of anyone with a different conception of this subject, the grand vizier said, and this, he concluded, pointing to the silver dish with the head of Ali Pasha Tepelena, was merely one more.

All afternoon, the square swarmed with crowds who hoped that the head, after its inspection by the members of the government, would finally be installed in the niche. They were still waiting in the evening. Apparently, the head required a prolonged medical examination.

Journalists, who had not been permitted access to the presentations of the head at either the Council of State or the Foreign Ministry, spent the entire night in the square, hoping to be present at the moment of its arrival. Abdulla knew most of them by name. Others returned to the square in the morning with swollen, sleepless eyes, to gather additional material for detailed features in their centerfolds. Foreign embassy employees darted through the crowd, evidently collecting data of a political nature, which was very easy to do on a day like this. Abdulla overheard snatches of careless conversation dropped by people without the slightest sense of responsibility. One said that no Albanian officials would be dismissed from their posts. "I don't believe it," someone replied. "After all that has happened, they're in serious trouble." "Still, there won't be any dismissals," another man insisted. "Perhaps not," replied the first. "The state takes a longer view." Blah-blah, thought Abdulla. Couldn't they hold this kind of conversation somewhere else? His eyes discerned among the crowd the deputy director of one of the capital city's leading banks. Abdulla recalled that the price of bronze had fallen yesterday, after news of the end of the war and the head's arrival in the city. At noon, they said, copper stocks would fall again. In recent years, Abdulla had noticed that it was easier to follow the fortunes of war in the fluctuating price of bronze than in the newspaper reports.

"What will happen to Albania now?" said someone under the very nose of the Keeper of Heads. Indeed, wondered Abdulla, what would happen to Albania? The question had been on everybody's lips recently, but was even more urgent for him, because it involved the fate of his elder brother, whose first letter had arrived at last. The letter was long, and described in detail the country in which he had been posted. There was a great plain in the northern part of Albania called the Plain of Kosovo, where, many centuries ago, the Ottoman army had conquered the insane peninsula of the Balkans in ten hours. According to his brother, on that June day the field was drenched with so much blood that its vegetation was changed for many years, either growing rampant or withering and dying. It was here, alas, that Sultan Murad I had been killed after the battle. Now, Abdulla's brother wrote, he himself was guarding the shrine that contained the sultan's tomb. In fact the emperor's body was not buried there, only his intestines. His body, without the innards, had been loaded on a camel armored with bronze plate and dispatched to the capital, deep in the heart of the kingdom. It is said that during a storm on the journey, lightning struck the camel carrying the dead sultan several times, but did no harm to either the camel or the body, because the bronze plates conducted the lightning into the earth in fiery forks like scarlet tassels.

So the martyred sultan also had two graves. Abdulla turned his head towards the niche. Just like you, he thought. They all had multiple graves and . . . multiple wives. But he himself, a week ago . . . his first wife . . . no doubt his last . . . and what was worse, not even with her . . . not even with her . . .

"What will they do to Albania now?" the same voice asked next to him. Poor people, Abdulla said to himself. Rather, what will they do to us? He stood for a moment as if numbed. It was one of those rare moments when he felt detached from himself, so that one part of him could judge the other. Since when do you think like this, he wondered. Since when have you changed sides? But his awareness of a divided self was fleeting, like his moment of rebellion. He soon became himself again, as listless and biddable as ever.

A few paces from the Traitor's Niche, Sefer the palace artist was hurriedly painting a picture of the severed head. The Islamic faith strictly forbade portraits of people, but Abdulla knew that the Court Protocol Section, after numerous applications to the Sheikh-ul-Islam, had finally obtained a license to depict severed heads. It had reasoned that these heads, as soon as they were placed in the niche of shame, were mere objects, and drawing them was no different to assembling a mosaic.

As always, people clustered around the painter. They stretched their necks in curiosity to look at the canvas and the colors, they whispered to one another and sometimes accidentally knocked the legs of the easel, but this did not bother the artist, who worked quickly, as if at any moment the cold might freeze his paints.

Eleven o'clock had still not struck, but Abdulla instinctively glanced towards Crescent Street, from where the doctor would arrive. It was the new head's first day and, according to the regulations, the doctor was obliged to inspect it and record its condition in a short report, in order to provide evidence should any complications arise later. It was also the doctor's duty to give his opinion on how long the head could remain in the niche.

He appeared at the crossroads at the precise moment when the clock on the tower of the Temple of the Ottoman Spirit struck eleven. He appeared as vivacious as ever, with a rolling gait and the usual smile, which was so constant that Abdulla was coming to believe that it was less an expression than a facial feature.

"Meetings," said the doctor while still some distance away. "Meetings all morning. Some people will not be persuaded that medicine makes progress like any other science. Good morning, Abdulla."

"Good morning, doctor," Abdulla said, bowing his head slightly.

"They start by opening old chronicles: this is how the glorious Timurtash was embalmed in the year such and such, this is how the blood was drained from the body of the Sheikh-ul-Islam in some other year, and so on. And the worst of it is, when you try to tell them about up-to-date methods, they turn on you with all kinds of political twaddle: doesn't Ali Pasha's head deserve a different kind of treatment to the head of the traitor Demirdag, a century ago? What answer is there to stupidity like that?" the doctor snorted. "Ah, here is our new friend," he burst out cheerfully, turning to the niche.

As Abdulla brought over the wooden ladder, their glances met.

"And what about you?" the doctor said, as if remembering something. "How's it going?"

Abdulla blushed and lowered his eyes.

"The same," he said.

A few weeks before, overcoming his terrible shyness, Abdulla had told the doctor the secret of the first nights of his marriage. It was a melancholy story. He was not having success with his young bride. The doctor had listened without the slightest surprise and this had encouraged Abdulla. "These things happen," the doctor had said. "You're neither the first nor the last." Then he'd asked Abdulla some questions.

Abdulla had found it difficult to answer them, especially the ones about his wife's body. The doctor had given him some advice and assured him that it was only temporary, caused mainly by the absence of women from everyday life.

"Hmm," the doctor said, setting his foot on the ladder. For a moment he screwed up his eyes, and then, looking straight at Abdulla, said, "Listen, you must try something else. You know what?"

The light went out of Abdulla's eyes. "What?" he asked in a faint voice.

"Visit a whore."

Abdulla raised his hand in protest.

"Never mind that," the doctor said, climbing the ladder. "My suggestion would fix it, dead sure."

Abdulla watched the heels of the doctor's shoes follow each other up the ladder. Those first nights had been endless hours of torture. "Don't worry," the doctor had told him. "It's all in the mind." Abdulla held his breath, not wanting to miss a word of what he said. "Desire becomes so strong," the doctor continued, "that at first it chokes itself." His words had swirled around Abdulla's head for the rest of the day. At times they seemed convincing, but still they were strange. Why should strong desire choke itself? And why did such a thing have to happen to him? He wondered if this were a punishment for some past sin. Should he perhaps not have pleasured himself, imagining his own aunt as he had once seen her in the bathroom through the keyhole?

The fourth night of his marriage had been a particular torture. The entire empire was on holiday celebrating the Night of Power. On that night, according to a centuries-old tradition, the sultan-emperor slept with a virgin. The capital city glittered with lights. Late in the evening, cannons were fired on the Tower of Drums, from the fortress of the prison and from the Admiralty, to mark the start of the Night of

Power. Abdulla lay stretched out alongside his young bride in the carefully warmed bedroom. Both were covered in cold sweat. The cannons resounded with increasingly horrific booms. Their barrels, the smoke, the gunpowder, the fire they spewed—all symbolized the manly vigor of the sultan, represented in iron and uproar. This earthquake shook the entire world, on which Abdulla crawled like a snail. He peered out of the corner of his eye at his bride's neck, which, stretched inertly over the pillow, so strangely tormented him, and he felt a faint throb of jealousy, bitter and sweet at the same time, that had recently become familiar. It was jealousy of the heads in the stone niche. Their lifeless eyes seemed to mock him. Bugrahan Pasha, the vizier of Trebizond, had had thirty-eight women in his harem, and his face was said to have turned yellow from endless orgies. Ali Pasha's second wife, Vasiliqia, was twenty-two years old, while the rebel vizier had been over eighty. They had all had so many wives, while he himself . . .

He felt betrayed. His body was slowly failing, about to give up. But the brunt of his anger was directed towards what had previously been his greatest joy: his cock. He could not forgive it. When he was not with his bride, when he was in the street or the café or even at the site of his sacred duty, it would unexpectedly swell and be ready for any exploit, but when he was with his wife it became flabby, shrank, and retreated like a puppy faced with a tiger. And so he cursed it for its treachery.

The doctor was clairvoyant. On the first day when Abdulla

had confided his anxiety, the doctor had asked appalling questions. Their second conversation had gone further still; Abdulla had never imagined that the day would come when someone would ask him if he'd ever seen a woman's private parts. He blushed in shame. "Listen," the doctor had said sternly, "if you want to get out of this mess, listen carefully to what I say. Otherwise go to those silly old women and have them undo the spell that's supposedly been laid on you. They'll make you swallow powdered ants and snake piss and crocodile balls and God knows what else, until you really do keel over."

The doctor had fixed his eyes upon him like a seer, until Abdulla admitted secrets that he had been sure he would carry to the grave. Yes, he had indeed seen a woman's private parts when he was a child, looking at his aunt through a keyhole. Strangely, this made no impression on the doctor, and it even struck him as totally normal. "Hmm, so you saw your aunt. Hmm, very good, very good. And now, tell me exactly, what was it like, or rather, what do you remember most?"

God forbid, Abdulla wanted to retort. How dare you talk about my aunt like this? But his tongue would not obey him, and betrayed him again. The overwhelming, most arresting impression was of a black bush . . . "Wait," interrupted the doctor. "Stop just there. Your bride, before her wedding night, no doubt shaved her little bush?"

Abdulla could not believe his ears. A stranger, in the middle of the café, after asking about his aunt's private parts, was now prying into his wife's. And he himself, her husband, instead of flying into a rage, striking him with the first implement that came to hand, sinking his teeth into his throat, and skinning him alive, was sitting and listening like some ninny. In his imagination he carried out all these acts of retaliation, and dragged the doctor through the square, in front of the appalled tourists, as far as the Obelisk of Tokmakhan or even to the entrance to the bank. But while he fantasized, from his mouth there came a lifeless yes.

"Ah," the doctor said, and banged the table so loudly that the old city news-criers sitting nearby turned to him in reproach. "Just what I thought. That's the answer to this riddle. Yes, it's just what I expected."

Before he offered his explanation, he mumbled some curses against the traditions of the country.

"It's a barbarous habit, Abdulla, don't you see? To shave a woman's bush is, I don't know what to say . . . it's like stealing the turban of the Sheikh-ul-Islam . . . do you understand? A black bush gives that little shrine all its attraction. It's the mystery, the darkness, the power of the night that drives us wild. It's what makes us truly mortal . . . don't you see?"

The doctor muttered to himself for a long time and then ordered a second coffee.

"Never mind," he said, brightening up. "There is some hope now. In your mind, a woman's private parts take the shape of a black patch. This is normal for any man. But on your wedding night, you were suddenly up against something bare and smooth, a sort of featherless bird, as you might call it. You poor soul, it's not your fault. In your position, I'm sure the same would have happened to me. I would have been totally unmanned. But now we have the key to this problem, and we can solve it. First thing, wait for her patch to grow again."

The doctor reckoned to himself: "Three weeks, an inch . . . five weeks . . . hmm. . . to put it briefly, in two months your marital shrine will be beautifully adorned . . . Why are you looking at me like that? Perhaps you're thinking, as our old saying goes, that it's like telling the goat to wait for the grass to grow. But there's nothing else you can do, Abdulla. It takes patience. Just wait, just wait."

He rubbed his hands, as if he, too, would be joining the celebration. Abdulla had never felt so spineless. Fortunately, the next time when the doctor had cheerfully asked him, "How's it going, Abdulla, is the forest growing?" he had looked so dejected that the doctor had not dared to tease him again.

Several weeks had passed since then. The place below his bride's belly grew dark, but instead of blossoming, Abdulla's hopes had almost entirely withered. The blind rage that seized him increasingly often was directed against his entire body. If this was how matters stood, and if the fire of his passion could never be lit again, wouldn't it be better to leave behind his body entirely? Cast aside forever his arms, legs, and wretched belly? Just as the defenders of a besieged fortress take vain refuge in its highest tower, shouldn't he retreat to his final hiding place, his head? If he were reduced merely to a head, his bride would have no reason to expect anything from him. Perhaps she would kiss him on the lips, with the real kiss of a woman, in the same way that the wife of the "blond pasha" had kissed her husband's head when it was brought to her. Abdulla thought he felt the slow movement of blood through his veins. To be only a head, in the stone niche. A sun that has set, with a never-ending aureole around his neck. Alone, facing the horror of the endless crowds of the capital city. A tyrant striking terror in the square, stared at by thousands of feverishly inflamed eyes. The center of the empire's attention. An extinguished star.

The murmuring in the square changed its tone. Abdulla raised his head and watched as the doctor descended and then steadied himself at the foot of the ladder, looking up pensively at the niche. All around them the crowd, which until then had followed the doctor's every movement with petrified attention, began to hum again. The Council of Ministers was in session once more, someone said. A cold wind blew around the square. The doctor kept staring at the niche. The white locks of the head fluttered and lay still. The honey must have frozen, Abdulla thought. The doctor shook his head two or three times. "Why?" he murmured as if in a dream. This head had tried to curl its lip at the entire empire, Abdulla thought wearily. He was slightly dizzy. The head's white hair seemed like mist. It occurred to Abdulla that only a few days ago a vizier's terrible pronouncements, with the power of life and death, had emerged from under these soft curls. When this beard had bristled, the empire had trembled. Now nothing was left but gentle wisps as soft as sheepskin. Abdulla thought of his bride's private parts, now also asleep. He had been unable to rouse them.

"The state hasn't seen an upheaval like this for years," the doctor said, pointing to the niche.

Abdulla didn't know how to answer. All the official statements had avoided the word *upheaval*. He could not tear his eyes from the niche. In what corner of this skull, he wondered, had the idea of rising up against this state first been born? It occurred to Abdulla that he had never rebelled against anything in this world, not even against his own self.

"See you soon, Abdulla," the doctor said, turning his eyes away from the niche.

Abdulla bowed. After a few steps, the doctor looked back.

"About that business, do as I told you," he called out, winking.

Abdulla felt himself blush.

A new wave of humanity flowed across the square. Parties of schoolchildren and members of religious communities came swarming down the Street of the Arms of Islam. No newspaper of the capital city could spread news as fast as the murmuring crowd. Phrases that Abdulla overheard became lodged in his memory like headlines, some in bold, others in small type. A state of emergency would be imposed not only in Albania but across a whole swathe of the Balkans. The search for Ali Pasha's treasure was continuing. Horrific discoveries were expected in the terrible dungeons of his castle. The next imperial courier would soon escort the rebel's widow, Vasiliqia, to the capital. The foreign minister, the *Reiz Efendi* . . .

Abdulla thought that the Fourth Directorate must have its agents dotted among the crowds in this square. You could hear the most astounding comments. Now, just a few paces away, under the very noses of the guards, two people were talking about what would happen to Albania. It would lose its privileges forever. "There's no doubt of that," one said, "but I'm curious to know, will they pronounce it a defiled land?" "I don't think so," the other man replied. "That's the slippery slope to hell." "And why don't you think so? Everyone is furious at the Albanians. Have you seen the newspapers? They say the Albanians have been indulged for long enough. Now they will drown in blood." "Everyone is against them now, I believe that," the second man said. "They were masters of the Balkans but now they've come to a bad end. All the rest who envied them their favors will have their chance for revenge now, that's understandable. Yet I still don't believe Albania will be destroyed. It's one of the most important defenses against the pressure of the Slavs. You'll see how they'll find a middle way, so that the Albanians will feel the state's anger but won't be totally wiped off the map. You said it yourself just now: the state takes a long view."

These fools again, thought Abdulla. Did they have nothing else to do but prattle on about the state's business? He didn't want to hear any more, but the voices were very close and forced their way into his ears. "What do you say—who will be appointed in Ali Pasha's place?" "That depends on the decree on the country's status. If it's declared a defiled land, then Hurshid Pasha might remain there. He's young and energetic. Or else . . ." "Or else what?" asked the first voice. "Or else, if the decree orders a milder regime, as I think it will, old Karadja Pasha might be posted there."

They went on talking about appointments, and it struck Abdulla that the busiest of the state ministries these days would surely be the Palace of Seals and Decrees. The fates of three thousand or so senior officials, of the state's one million employees, depended directly on this palace, whose heavy columns appeared dusted with old gold.

This palace appointed viziers, the two commanders-in-chief of the European and Asian divisions of the army, the pashas of the land and the pashas of the sea. All we need are pashas of the air, Abdulla thought anxiously, but confident all the same that human greed would not extend to envying the angels their place in heaven. Important and dramatic decrees issued from the palace, like beasts with claws and manes leaping out of a thundery black sky: the Decree of Defilement, the Decree of Caw-caw, the Decree of War, the Black Decree, which left your name as filthy as soot, the Decree of Clemency, which left you with your head, and the Decree of Death, which took it away. Compared with these, all other decrees seemed gentler, like cats beside lions. Strangely, the decrees on taxes, land rent, water, salt, customs, and the devaluation of the currency were issued from the same gate, as were other orders, instructions, and rulings on individual salaries, perquisites, and internments, and on the place of each person in the Council of State, at celebrations, at official dinners, and finally in the state cemetery.

Abdulla had learned all these things piecemeal, day after day, on the square by the Traitor's Niche. At first, such information had been jumbled in the confused muttering of the crowd, like stone and debris on a construction site. Then a clear outline had slowly emerged, creating in Abdulla's mind an image of the whole edifice of the state.

But after the initial shock of amazement, when he thought that nothing more perfect than this magnificent structure could exist on earth or in heaven, Abdulla had sensed perpetual squabbling within it. This discovery had grieved him, but later he had recognized that the state had been inured to this bickering for centuries. Neither the rivalry between the secular and religious powers, nor the struggles among castes and provinces, whose echo barely reached him, nor the rumors and grudges, nor even the secret plots that were discovered time and again, did anything to diminish the majesty of the state. This was because the terrible sultan-emperor, Allah's regent on earth, stood over everything, above the two branches of power and above all the castes, and listened. Abdulla was reassured to some degree by this, but still wondered why there were such bitter quarrels. But whenever he asked this question, his thoughts stopped short as if on the brink of a precipice. His mental resources stretched only this far. Nor did the murmuring on the square, which covered every possible topic, provide any answer. At such times, Abdulla imagined the mechanisms of the state as huge mill wheels turning with a muffled creak in the darkness, dripping black water from the empire's eight-centuries-old foundations. It was impossible to make out anything in this gloom.

The word *bronze* caught Abdulla's ear amid the din and seemed to cast a ray of light on the mystery, but its gleam was so pale that it expired instantly. Sometimes things that had once seemed totally innocent awoke his mistrust. Ordinary words to do with the price of salt, customs duties, and the new law on the banks and interest rates troubled his conscience. Sometimes he went so far as to suspect that the decrees that seemed as gentle as kittens were like drops of water eroding rock, or a wife's whispering that sparks her husband's jealousy, and in fact prepared the way for those other decrees, weighty, majestic, and bloody, whose promulgation made the whole world tremble.

This chilled Abdulla's soul more than anything, and he silently cursed the strangers whose voices had planted in him these doubts. What bastards they were, what demons with their mad ranting. Then he cursed his own imagination and quickly thought of calm and stately things: the procession of official carriages on feast days, the little lights on the four minarets of Hagia Sophia, the marble tombs of high dignitaries and the bathhouses where their wives washed their abdomens, no doubt adorned with precious gems, and especially these grandees' heavy testicles, hanging like cheeses in muslin, with their rigid cocks in between.

High-level officials in particular spurred Abdulla's imagination. He couldn't tell if he was frightened or allured. Probably both.

And now one of them, Ali Tepelena, had died, and this entire caste was shaken as if by an earthquake. Lights would surely blaze until midnight in the Palace of Seals and Decrees. That was where everything was decided. There would be transfers of officials in all the remotest corners of this immense empire. These men would fight like wolves, stripping the richest provinces of their wealth, clawing at one another for official posts, writing anonymous letters.

Whereas Abdulla, a lowly civil servant whose misfortune had been to learn the taste of power here on the edge of this square, like someone who gets drunk from the mere smell of the brandy still, would never have any dealings with this palace. The only kind of decree for him would be a death sentence. Here in the Traitor's Niche would be placed . . . the head of Black Abdulla, who rebelled against the state.

Abdulla shook himself and straightened his back. The roar of the square grew louder. Fragments again reached his ears like headlines. The whole western part of the Balkans was on military alert. Greece had taken advantage of Ali Tepelena's uprising, and made its own moves. In high circles it was whispered that V.V., the minister of finance, the new guardian of Black Ali's young widow, intended to seek her hand in marriage. Others said that the senior official Halet, whose wife had died of breast cancer two months before, would do this. There were rumors that the Qyprili family would fall, alongside Albania. A magnificent welcome was predicted for the victorious Hurshid Pasha, the hero of the hour, on his return to the capital next week. His career would surely soar to dizzy heights. He might even become grand vizier. The price of bronze would subside again by midday . . . and Abdulla's member, too.

The Keeper of Heads smiled sourly to himself. The hero of the hour, he thought. In the smart cafés, young men had started to wear their beards in "Hurshid style." Ladies of distinction no doubt dreamed of him. Perhaps Abdulla's wife did, too. For a while Abdulla's eyes stared blankly, and then a strange light flickered across them, as swift as a marten.

5

The Frontier of the Empire.
Cloudy Day

A SLOW FIELD cart drawn by oxen wandered erratically across the half-frozen mire. Here and there depleted haystacks, consumed by passing army horses or rotting in the rain, seemed to have drawn silently closer together, resembling ragged ghosts taking refuge now that the battles and mayhem were over. After a day of tumult the wind had dropped and fat sodden clouds now hung in the sky. The occasional rumble of thunder boomed, gone as soon as it was perceptible, like some drowned corpse.

Under the leaden sky, in all the villages and towns of the newly subjugated territory, news-criers read out the sultan's decree that had arrived from the capital city: "To all slaves and bondsmen of the great sultan, subjects of the province of Albania, governed until recently by Black Ali. Your lives are spared. You will eat in peace the bread of slavery, if you surrender your weapons immediately. You are ordered to take off all clothes of bright colors and to dress only in black or gray homespun. Do not let your hair grow, and cover your heads with a fez of black ox-skin. Do not ride on stallions, mares, or mules. Block up your chimneys, so that your smoke no longer rises to the sky but leaves your houses through the doors and windows, having first blackened with soot your chattels and livestock and children. All these punishments will be lifted only when you prove to the great sultan by your deeds that you have banished from your souls the demon of rebellion and put aside all memory of Black Ali."

People standing by house gates, beside fields, and at inn doorways listened in bewilderment and said nothing. They did not speak even when the news-crier turned his back and set off for the next village. With tight lips, they turned their heads towards the fields, left barren by the war, as if they might find there some further explanation of this new decree. Flocks of ravens and magpies swirled over the dark earth pocked with shell holes, here and there forming crazy patterns. It was sufficient for people to look at the vast expanse of soft, black, tormented soil with its blighted crops. Everyone knew what a wife's miscarriage meant, and so could easily grasp the disaster of a miscarriage of the harvest. The mere sight of this neglected land was enough to show that a calamity had already happened. This decree added nothing to it, just as the jabbering of magpies added nothing to the grief of the winter earth.

Some decrees were old, drawn from the ancient files of the Central Archive or copied from them almost word for word. Others were sloppily drafted by seventy-year-old officials, haphazardly adapted to the times and the different provinces of the immense state. People were used to these sorts of decrees. For centuries, news-criers had come and gone, but little had changed in the Albanian territories. The sky and the earth were there, sometimes in harmony with each other and sometimes not, bringing fat years or lean years. The sun played its part and so did the moon, always remote from everything, and finally there was the sultan, somewhere far away at the center of the world, who sent all serious catastrophes and turned upside down the earth beneath your feet and the sky above your head. For this reason the rancor against him was age-old and instinctive, as if he were an aspect of the weather or of the mountain crags and the clouds above them. The British consul liked to say at receptions that unexpected things might happen if someone discovered how to gather these clouds of wrath. Reportedly, Halet the official answered that it was not as easy as gathering cotton.

At that time Ali Pasha's rebellion had not yet been overt, although there were rumors everywhere of its imminent outbreak. Clearly the British consul was trying to measure the pulse of the government, thinking of the storms to come.

The approach of thunder was palpable. The government met every day. The ancient Palace of Psst-Psst, the War Ministry, the Fourth Directorate of the Interior Ministry, the Foreign Ministry, and the Palace of Dreams, all these ponderous mechanisms of the state worked overtime. Everyone was on tenterhooks.

But the most recent communiqués from the province indicated that, against all predictions, that old lion Ali Pasha had not succeeded in concentrating Albania's ancient resentment. He had risen against the sultan purely out of a personal grudge.

"Hear ye, all slaves and bondsmen of the sultan," the news-criers still called, their throats hoarse in the icy air. "Now that the war is over . . ."

Ali Tepelena had risen up alone against his sovereign, like Kara Mahmud Bushatli and other crazy pashas of Albania before him. These pashas were insanely audacious; the Venetians said that they had the devil in their belly and merely itched to enter battle, for any reason. So when the sultan failed to summon them to the "great field of arms," they lost their tempers and took up arms against him or, not knowing what else to do, launched confused attacks on neighboring foreign states, Venice, Austria, or whoever stood in their way.

Ali Pasha resembled them in many ways, but was greater in every respect, and was also wise instead of mad. Yet the Albanians did not take him into their hearts. Although he was of their blood, he had oppressed them for years, like some Turkish vizier or worse. He had ordered them to hang, forced them to dance on thorns, put them in irons, humiliated and impaled them. So when he confronted the sultan and was forced to call on their aid, they made no move. They had gone to wars all their lives as easily and naturally as to weddings in autumn, but they did not respond. Let these tyrants quarrel with each other. They can gouge out each other's eyes and pull out each other's beard. Why should we care?

War drew closer. The messengers of the vizier (still known to his own people as Ali Pasha but to his enemies as Black Ali, as though night for him had already fallen) struggled blindly through the winter dusk. In their saddlebags they carried official seals, shackles, and gold sovereigns, but none of these were of any use. People paid no attention.

Then appeared the first carts of the campaign, the infantry caravans and wet artillery, the staff headquarters with flags with the crescent moon and quotations from the Qur'an, the logistics units behind the lines, the musicians, executioners, peddlers. For the last four hundred years, they had been coming again and again like a recurring nightmare.

When this rabble had wrapped itself around the walls of his castle, Ali Tepelena issued a final appeal to his fellow countrymen: look, they are here. But still no response came. The Albanians began to forget about him. They were more worried about the shell holes and cart ruts in the fields, the haystacks nibbled by passing artillery mules, than by the fate of Ali Pasha. And so they left him to himself with his personal guards and cannons.

Even when it was clear that Ali's end was near, the usual time for remorse, the Albanians' regrets were of a mild and general nature. They felt some sympathy for him because of his great age, for neither the country's epics nor the state chronicles recorded another rebellious vizier of eighty-two, and also because of the painful desertion of his sons and grandsons, all pashas and noblemen themselves, who rallied to the sultan. However, they felt pity less for him than for themselves and their land, and disappointment after a quarter-century of hope. The land slowly but relentlessly began to make its own reproaches, filling the shell holes and trenches this war had gouged in its surface, and the Albanians, too, began to repair whatever they could in their fields, and within themselves.

The news-criers were still traveling the rime-covered roads, but people were familiar with their old stories. Nobody would seriously be forced to change their clothing. The Albanians would mount their horses as before and wear their hair as they liked, and smoke would climb from chimneys straight or crooked, as it pleased.

They were less surprised by the news-criers than by the wild ducks that came in March, and which this year were very early. But this war had also come at an unusual time, in the depths of winter.

After the suppression of the rebellion the world seemed deadened. The croaking of ravens sounded louder, especially to the ears of the army's sappers who studied their flight, in the hope that the birds might point them towards unburied corpses under the layer of frost.

The young woman's long black skirt rustled on the ground, and as it passed it gathered dust, pebbles, and sometimes half-burned cartridges. Ali Pasha's twenty-two-year-old widow wandered through the vaults of her occupied castle, followed by her two women-in-waiting, an architect, and an employee of the Interior Ministry dressed as a dervish. The entourage walked in total silence behind her long shadow, slackening or quickening their pace according to hers, stopping when she did and setting off again as soon as she moved on. Throughout this silent progress the whole party, except for the ministry's employee, maintained the same distance.

They were looking for the rest of the treasure of the defeated vizier, which remained undiscovered. They accompanied the widow through the chambers and crypts in the hope of prompting a recollection of suspicious repairs or traces of unexpected plasterwork.

Immediately after Ali's head had been sent to the capital, his treasure had followed, escorted by a nine-hundred-strong guard. But in response, instead of any expression of thanks or even pleasure at the gold and jewels, there arrived, in haste, a deputy director of the Imperial Bank. People who saw him descending from his carriage were astonished first to see certain long shapes emerging from the door of the vehicle, followed by a person. These elongated objects turned out to be his legs, followed by his torso, and at last his head. The banker demanded to be taken at once to Hurshid Pasha in order to inform him that long and complicated calculations (Allah, said Hurshid Pasha to himself, when had they found the time for these calculations?) had shown that not all of Black Ali's treasure had been rendered, and the capital city demanded the remaining part at once. Hurshid Pasha's hands turned cold. Then, when he had collected enough saliva to speak, he declared to this contemptible scrivener that he would issue a special order for the rest of the treasure to be found without fail, if it really was incomplete. As he pronounced these few words, a question crawled through one of the lower strata of his brain. Why were such spindly creatures as this sinister banker allowed to wander the surface of the earth, and even deliver state communiqués? Distractedly, he thought that all the evils of the world were caused by people who were either very short or very tall. Then, when this man had left, Hurshid Pasha gave an order for all the prisoners of the castle to be put to torture, and he asked for the widow of the defeated pasha to be brought to his tent. On the direct instruction of the Sublime Porte, she was to leave for the capital that same day.

Hurshid Pasha had heard about Vasiliqia, but had never seen her. Black Ali had never attended any state dinners after he married her. She was pretty, but not as beautiful as he had imagined. Nevertheless, he would have taken her with pleasure into his harem, or even as his wife, for who had more right to do this than the man who had made her a widow? However, the mighty Directorate of Protocol had stretched out its hand to seize her.

Vasiliqia looked him straight in the eye, frankly and without the hatred or even the awe that the sight of her husband's conqueror might be expected to inspire in her. At any other time, Hurshid Pasha would have known how to reward this indifference, but his thoughts were elsewhere. There was no thrill to their confrontation. For him, it was no longer ardent or arousing, for the simple reason that he, her husband's vanquisher, was also his successor and lord over everything that was his, including Vasiliqia. Hurshid Pasha set aside this aspect, as well as his own youth, for he was a pasha of only forty-two, and said to her in a voice that seemed strange even to himself, "Listen, sister . . . my daughter . . ."

He spoke gently about general matters, including the treasure, but without threats or entreaties, and without pity, in the tones of an equal. The widow sometimes nodded assent, and at the end of the meeting added nothing but a final yes.

The carriage that was to carry the woman to the capital had been waiting outside the fortress gates since morning. Whether the treasure was found or not, the carriage would set off on its long journey that afternoon.

Wandering the labyrinth of the castle, Vasiliqia thought of Hurshid Pasha's trim beard with its pale, bronze-colored glint, like a lamp emitting its last gleams before it is quenched. This beard glittered all the more when its owner spoke of gold, silver, and bronze coins. "You are young," he had said, "and when you go to the capital, you will surely have prompt offers of marriage from eminent men of religion and the state. Yes, yes, plenty of them," he continued, studying his fingernails. At this moment she thought that he was about to make his own proposal. But he did not. He repeated that she was young and said that her husband's bad name did not stain the reputation of his wife. On the contrary, his character, reflected in his wife, was purged of its coarser features and regained its true brilliance.

Vasiliqia paused at a wide embrasure in one corner of the

castle and stared out at the frost-covered plain. This winter had frozen the whole world. For an entire week, not a ray of sunlight had penetrated the heavy gray dough of the sky. She couldn't believe the sun would ever shine again. Had they cut off the plain at the horizon, just as they had severed her husband's head at the shoulders?

She shut her eyes but opened them again at once, because closing her eyes put her in greater danger. She started walking again and the entourage followed her rustling skirts in total silence. The corridors were as cold as ice, and the alcoves and walls patched with damp as if an entire army of snails had crawled over them. Occasionally she examined one of these patches, and the eyes of the Interior Ministry employee and the architect followed hers. The two men behind her moved aside and made notes on a sheet of paper.

Vasiliqia's eyes were large, and through them, as if through some crevice, one could see her mind straining to remember. Sometimes the pupils swung to one side, as if they would dive into her head and not reappear again, leaving the hollows of her eyes a blank and lifeless white. Then they would turn back at the last moment and slowly straighten. When this happened, the architect made a special note on his paper, and the two men's hopes of finding the rest of the treasure increased.

In fact, Vasiliqia was not looking for the lost part of the treasure but for her murdered husband. It seemed to her that somewhere in the walls and corners she would discover the hidden part of him.

They hadn't been married for long and she hadn't known him well. He had spent a lot of time with her recently, during the siege. Otherwise she might not have gotten to know him at all. But in these past months, when Hurshid Pasha's army had encircled them as if they were in a pit, she had been alone with him for days. She had heard that it had been like this at the beginning of Ali's life, when he was only eighteen and his mother married him to the kittenish little Um Gulsumi, who was even younger than himself. The young couple had sat alone together for hours on end. But between these wives lay sixty years of his life that belonged to no one. On occasion Vasiliqia had tried to encroach on this territory, but she felt lost as soon as she took her first steps into it, as if in a temple belonging to another world. Terrified, she had turned back. But in the last few months, the sphinx had begun to talk.

That late-autumn night had been moonless, with only a few distant stars, scattered by the wind across the empty sky. Ali and his wife were lying together in one of the chambers of the castle's western tower, from which a part of the autumn sky could be seen.

"I'll go to war against the sultan," he said to her in a pensive voice.

At first she said nothing. Only after a pause, not taking her eyes away from the distant shimmer of the stars, she asked softly, "Against the sultan and emperor?"

He nodded more with his beard than with his head.

"The sultan is the light of the world," she said, and at that moment felt his breathing grow faster.

"I'll put out that light."

He seemed to puff out these words, rather than pronounce them.

She half closed her eyes. How wonderful, she thought, not knowing why it should be so fine. She listened to his breathing and slowly the reason dawned on her. It was a horribly wonderful thing for a woman lying in the marital bed one autumn night to hear her husband say not "I'll put out the light," as hundreds of thousands of husbands do before lovemaking and sleep, but, just as calmly and naturally, "I'll put out the light of the world."

"It will be dark," she said, more to encourage him to speak than to object.

"I know," he said shortly. She calmly stroked his beard and whispered, breathing into his ear, "But why will you do this?"

At first he remained silent. In the low light shed by the candle in its copper sconce, she noticed that his beard, eyes, and eyebrows were caught in a grimace, and the reasons for the war lay in that distorted expression. He was trying to express these reasons, but apparently could not do so, and so he replied simply, "You won't be able to understand."

She was not at all offended. Her hand continued gently stroking his beard, the way he liked. "Why do you want to climb higher?" she whispered as she caressed him. "Why not climb down a little? Wouldn't it be more natural to yield, to be more human, rather than overreaching to become more than a man?" Of course, it was wonderful to lay your head beside a husband's head that contained reasons for war, and even the decision to start one, and yet, and yet, wasn't it a totally insubstantial kind of pleasure?

Sometimes she caught herself thinking it was her own fault when, lying on their soft bed, she felt she was merely an unconsidered woman rather than his wife. You're married to him, she told herself, the most powerful man after the sovereign in this empire that stretches across three continents. Never forget this. But the thought of being his wife gave her only a cold and distant joy that she could not grasp, a glittering but slippery joy, like a crystalline mineral in a dream. *The vizier growls like thunder* . . . a song about him started. How well these words described him, she thought. More than a pasha, a minister, a man of flesh and bone and gray hair, he was a thunderclap. Sometimes she thought that she had married a mountain laden with an entire winter's burden of snow. Lightning, thunder, and the silvery light of snow had become her jewelry, but could she hang these around her neck? She yearned for an ordinary wedding with guests from some mountain valley in black trousers, with red tassels bobbing like little flames on their sandals, white horses and rifle fire, and the Roma with their wedding tambourines. Her longing grew and entwined itself around the towers of the castle. She thrust it away, telling herself that fate had given her a different life at the side of a mighty husband. She was the wife of this thunderbolt, ruling over men just as the weather governs the world.

But had he really been so powerful? She had not asked herself this question during the week after his death, even in her most secret thoughts. The question arose of its own accord, or a pale suggestion of it secretly crept up on her, calmly gleaming and biding its time. With it came the memory of his body dragged down the staircase, his back arched, his arms useless behind him, his head striking the treads, and then his arms, his back falling onto the next tread, and then his head, and his arms behind him hitting the stairs in their turn. What a long time his descent took until, on the final stair, the great stroke of a shining yataghan cut the world in two.

She had watched all this from ten paces away, unable to shut her eyes. A curse on you for not closing, she had thought in the days that followed, addressing her own eyes in the mirror. Why had they stayed open, when the sky itself should have gone dark to hide the sight of that calamity?

So this is how you die, she thought when his head fell on the next stair while his arms still trailed behind. You wanted to amaze the world with your death. She had stared at him, sure that a miracle would happen and he would stand up again to keep his promise, but his back fell on another stair while his head thudded against the next and an arm flailed over his face. "I trust you and I trust death," he had often said in the last few weeks, when he had lost all hope. "They can't take you or death away from me." She had sat totally naked in the cold light of the moon, and he had stared at her, repeating over and over for hours: "Neither of you." She expected him to stand up on the second-to-last stair, and thought she saw his arm leaning against the tread for support, but then the head fell and everything, body and arms, crumpled in a heap and it was all over. Her last thought before she fainted was that he'd been left with nothing, not with the death he wanted, not with her . . . nothing . . .

The widow stared at the patches and trails of damp, some large and others small. There was no end to the castle's chambers, and the cold froze her to the marrow. So part of the treasure is missing, she thought vaguely. Something was always missing. She was looking for her husband. There had always been a part of him missing.

Soon they would come to the great hall of arms. She had found him there one day as he sat brooding, absorbed by some copper trinkets. His architect and one of the most famous painters of Janina had just left the hall. "What are these things?" she had asked him, noticing the disks that did not resemble either women's jewelry or men's medals. He laughed, but coldly, in the style of the unresponsive disks. "It's just as you say," he said, "they aren't jewelry or medals. They're the state emblems."

"State emblems?" She stared at him in puzzlement. "But we already have those. They were decided by the great sultans long ago." Then he told her that these would be the emblems of the new state. He talked slowly and gravely and she listened openmouthed. Then she understood: he wanted to found an Albanian state. Creating a state was to her mind a terrible, unimaginable thing, like giving birth to an entire world. Just as they say that new heavenly bodies are fashioned from old cosmic dust, so the new world of Albania was to be formed from the dust of the old Ottoman universe, from that constellation of terrors and crimes, postprandial poisonings, nighttime assassinations, monks holding lanterns in the rain, dervishes with knives and messages hidden in their hair, from that profusion of rebellious pashas, bureaus with thousands of files, informers, outlawed viziers and "black" pashas with a price on their heads who swarmed like ghosts before or after death—all the rotting debris of empire.

"Created?" she interrupted him gently. Hadn't it once existed? Didn't Scanderbeg create such a thing? (She pronounced his name very softly, like any word one was forbidden to utter in public.) Still he frowned, as he always did when he heard this name. He continued as gloomily as before. Although Albania had existed at one time, it had been destroyed, and had crumbled away four hundred years ago. Now he wanted to re-create it in the midst of this present hell.

He cracked his fingers repeatedly. Unlike on other occasions when they had talked about his fame, this conversation annoyed him beyond measure.

"It's so difficult, so hard," he said at last and, unusually for him, sighed, staring at the book by Machiavelli that lay on the oak table and which had been read to him recently at dinner.

The hall of arms was as cold as ever, with that dazzling

northern light. Why didn't he succeed, she wondered. Who was stopping this man who stopped at nothing? The sultan? Hadn't he said how easily he would crush the old scoundrel?

"So who's stopping you?" she finally asked, timorously.

He turned around abruptly, as if that "who" were a mouse that had scuttled out of the corner of the room and had to be crushed at once.

The northern light was now behind his back, feeble, as if filtered and through the fringe of a blanket.

"Who's stopping me?" he said. "Who's stopping me? Nobody."

These last words, although uttered in a low voice, came out in a howl. This was typical of his speech, which sounded so placid on the surface, but concealed an inner roar.

"Albania itself is stopping me," he murmured. "Nothing else."

Vasiliqia understood very little of what he said. She sensed only that the conversation should be brought to an end at once. But later, when he began talking again, Vasiliqia began to grasp what he meant. He groaned and complained that Albania itself crumbled in his hands. He couldn't get hold of it. It was like those glowworms that leave a phosphorescent gleam on your fingers if you touch them, but nothing else.

She had seen wandering gypsies who, with a magic piece of iron called a magnet, compelled fragments of metal, nails, and filings. Apparently, in a similar way, these mountains, muddy fields, rains, words, people, and clouds would have to be drawn together and transformed from the raw dough of a world into something called "the Albanian state." But he did not possess the magic to do this. His power had extended to everything—terror, palaces, bridges, wars, diplomacy—but not his mother country.

The sketches of the flag and the state emblems lay in the hall of arms, but it seemed that no state would come together there.

This became clearer to Vasiliqia as she drew closer to her husband in the weeks that followed. Her husband secretly envied Scanderbeg of the Kastriots, the creator of the Albanian state of long ago. Four hundred years before, at the age of thirty, Scanderbeg had done something that now seemed impossible: on the ruins of an old Albanian state, destroyed by the quarrels of its princes and the Turkish onslaught, he had rebuilt his country. But for Ali Pasha it was too late. He was over eighty, and the rebuilding of Albania was still a long way off. He envied still more keenly the future statesman who would accomplish this impossible task. Scanderbeg was in the past, and this statesman was in the future, and he himself stood between them, a thundering vizier whose place in history nobody could predict. How fine it is when the skies resound to your thunder, as the song said about him. But he would retort that thunderclaps didn't last long and came only at the turn of the seasons. He wanted something more.

He had first talked to Vasiliqia about immortality after an English poet called Byron visited their castle. This was the first and only man with whom she had betrayed him.

It was a betrayal without shape, words, sight, or substance, like the setting of the moon. He was handsome, with a limp, and nearer her own age. He was a pasha in his own country (there called lords) and he wrote verses like Haxhi Sherreti. He stayed two days in the castle of Tepelena and on the third he set off on the road to Greece. All this time, the wind hissed like a snake and crawled on its belly, before lifting its head at some distant crossroads. Vasiliqia had sat miserably by one of the south-facing windows and caught herself thinking about the poet. Oh God, look after him, she said to herself. He was so young and good-looking, and his poetry made him appear almost transparent, whereas down south, where he was headed, there were so many coarse, bearded men sunk in bloody crime. Her husband found her like this, with eyes fixed on the distance. He could tell what she was thinking. "It's true," he said, "he set off late, but nothing will happen to him. He's one of the immortals." He uttered these last words with sarcasm; he refused to believe that poems could make anyone immortal. Verses were like the herbs of embalmers: useful in preserving the bodies of great men. They had no value in themselves.

One day (after he had proclaimed the uprising and also declared an Albanian state), as if remembering her question in the hall of arms, he took her down to the castle dungeon, to show her his enemies. In just this way, at the beginning of their marriage, he had shown her his property, his stables of thoroughbred horses, the little fortresses on the sea coast, the ring sent by Bonaparte, and his mother's will. As she walked behind him, she said, "So we'll see the secret chambers of the state." Why hadn't she realized before that beneath where they lived there were people bound in irons?

The dungeon was a pit roofed by a stone vault, which appeared to sway and shake in the light of the torches with their choking stench. When their eyes cleared they saw the chains fixed to the wall a little below the height of a man. They were short, and did not allow a prisoner to stretch out on the ground. The men hung half suspended, with knees slightly bent and backs leaning against the wall, or turned to the sides. Some had their heads and chests jutting forward, their waists restrained by iron bands. One, entirely fastened to the wall, looked like a bas-relief.

Ali Pasha stopped in front of this last man.

"Do you understand now that you were wrong?" he said to him. In the airless cellar, words fell to the ground as soon as they left a human mouth.

The bas-relief didn't move. The guard brought the torch close to its head and Ali Pasha called out:

"Speak, or are you dead?"

Still the bas-relief didn't move.

"No, he's not dead," the guard said.

"Up above, I've made Albania an independent state," Ali Pasha said, "but you won't see it."

Ali Pasha did not take his eyes off the human form, pressed against the dungeon wall as if against an anvil. He waited a few moments until the bas-relief moved. First one shoulder, then part of the man's back, and finally his head detached themselves from the stone and mortar. The shape slowly turned to face the pasha and stared rigidly at him.

"So," Ali Pasha said, "do you understand now?"

"Hahaha," went the prisoner. In the open air it might have been a laugh, but down here it was only a muffled fall of dust.

"Hahaha," the prisoner went again. "You've done nothing up there." He paused for a moment. As he talked, he indeed shook dust and mud from his hair.

"You've done nothing," he repeated, "for you're still a pasha."

"But how do you know that I'm still a pasha? I've become what you call a *leader*." He uttered the word with contempt, with a protracted "*ea*." "A *leader*," he repeated. "Do you hear?"

Instead of answering, the prisoner rattled his chains. "Pasha," he muttered between his teeth. "My hands can tell what you are. This is not the way to make Albania." His words came in fragments, from the grave, covered in earth. "You might create a fief, but not a state . . . Albania won't follow you . . . No. You'll be all alone . . ."

"Shut up," Ali cried.

"You've climbed onto a blind horse, Ali."

"Shut your mouth!"

"Albania isn't your mother, Hanko."

"Beat him," Ali shouted.

The guard, thinking it would take too long to pass the torch to his left hand and take out his pistol with his right to hit him with its butt, struck him on the face with the torch instead. The flame flared, and sparks and ash fell to the ground. There was a smell of burned hair. The head fell back, and the body slumped and flattened itself against the wall. The prisoner became a bas-relief again.

Vasiliqia wanted to throw up.

This prisoner had said these very words at a meeting of the vizier's council: "Our Albanian state, if we create it, will be made by an Albanian leader and not a pasha." "What do you mean by this?" Ali had interrupted. "Are you going to lead the state yourself, since I'm a pasha?" "Not at all," the man replied. "My liege, you may put yourself at the head of the state, but you'll have to turn yourself from a pasha into a leader." "But I am a leader, among other things," Ali butted in. "No, my liege," the other man went on, again addressing him with this archaic word used by the first counts and princes of Arbëria. "Right now you're only a pasha, and to become a leader you must cease to be a pasha." "Hahaha," Ali laughed, "what sort of riddle is this?" "It's not a riddle, my liege, I'm telling you the simple truth. Leave off being a pasha, become a leader, and all Albania will love you. Do it before it's too late, my liege. Otherwise Albania won't follow you." "Enough," Ali howled. "Put him in chains."

It was the words themselves that had been clamped in irons.

Emerging from the prison into daylight, Vasiliqia felt faint. You've climbed onto a blind horse, she repeated to herself as her knees gave way. Albania won't follow you, no.

Ali Pasha's face was lemon yellow. Vasiliqia knew that the prisoner had opened an old wound. Despite her husband's efforts to conceal it, his envy of Scanderbeg was obvious. Albania had followed Scanderbeg, and not for one year or two but for twenty-five years and more—twenty-five years in his lifetime plus eleven years after his death. And Albania was still ready to follow his ghost, more prepared to follow this phantom than the living Ali Pasha.

As the months passed, Ali Pasha's correspondence with the sultan petered out. The sovereign's letters grew more curt and the final salutations were briefer, like fur coats that had once had a magnificent sheen and were now dull and moth-eaten. Courtesies were slowly and pitilessly stripped away, and the naked truth, concealed for years on end, was exposed.

Ali Pasha knew that bad times lay ahead and dispatched couriers to the four corners of the country to summon help from the provinces before the storm broke. But the couriers came back without word, only the clattering of their horses' hooves. Their dust-covered faces looked blank and smelled of nothing. Nothing from the north or the west. Ali Pasha sent threats, then kind words, then threats again, but this same dusty nothingness came back.

Albania had not listened. "What a feeble country," he muttered, pacing up and down the hall of arms. "Albania has grown old, deaf, no longer fit to fight." But he said this only to ease his grief. It was a very bitter thing to admit that Albania had ears but pretended not to hear.

"I've committed crimes," he said time and again to Vasi-liqia during their long nights together, which were as chill and lifeless as wax. "But show me a ruler without crimes on his hands. Hanko, my mother, God rest her soul, pushed me into some of them." He talked to her about his mother, and Vasiliqia thanked destiny that her mother-in-law had died before she had even been born. In quiet moments, his crimes crowded upon his mind. He told her about spine-chilling murders, prisons dripping with blood, peasants forced to dance barefoot on thorns, the slaughter at the inn at Valarea. When his cheeks grew tense and his nose sharper (sometimes this nose seemed to stretch in the shape of a coffin down his long face), she could guess which of his exploits he had brought to mind. But crimes were not the most important thing, he explained to her. All the other nobles, the Balshajs, the Topiajs, and the glorious Kastriots, had prisons and chains. There must be another reason why Albania had not followed him.

He thought he could hear horses' hooves. But almost all the messengers had already come home. There were a few latecomers from the most distant provinces, but the sound of their horses from afar told him that they brought nothing.

They won't listen to me. They've abandoned me, he said to himself, his jaw clenched. At one time, a simple horn call brought them to battle, but now all my thousand bell towers won't rouse them. They're as deaf as sacks of wool.

Then his rage subsided and he judged more calmly. He realized that Albania was taking its revenge. For forty years, addicted to his own power and fame, he had more or less forgotten her. For him Albania had been an estate, with decrees, taxes, and laws: not the country of Albania, but a prime dominion of the empire. Before he was a rebel leader, he had been a great landowner, a pasha with vast estates. Better than any bookkeeper, he knew about profits and percentages, currency rates, land rents. No, it was not just the prisons that kept him at odds with Albania. There were other explanations. He had a bigger army than Scanderbeg, more artillery, equipment, money, land. And yet Albania had followed Scanderbeg at his very first summons. What had been his appeal? he brooded, as if Albania were a woman. Nobody dared give him an answer, so he read and reread the secret reports that contained all the grumbling against him. The reports told him that Scanderbeg had possessed less artillery, but had greater ideas. What ideas? Tell me, for God's sake. And because there was no reply, Ali Pasha went on arguing with himself. Rather tell me I've become a burden to the earth. He leafed through the dispatches again, and continued to take issue with them. So Scanderbeg changed the course of history? So he turned Albania towards the West? Was history a cart, and Albania, too, to be turned around in the middle of the road? And hadn't Ali Pasha also risen against the sultan? But a pitiless voice whispered that while he had indeed risen against the sultan, it was for personal reasons, because of a personal offense, because he suspected that the sultan might overthrow him . . . Besides, he had marched against the sultan by himself, friendless.

The newspapers were increasingly using this word, which he detested. You left me friendless by deserting me, he thought. You left me alone like a beggar. He knew how the Albanians would reply, if they had a voice: You made yourself a beggar. Just as you abandoned us, we abandoned you. And they would no doubt mention his estate. According to them, he had neglected everything for the sake of his estate. Take away my estate, he might reply. You've complained about it for years. I wasn't going to waste it on myself, I kept it for you. Look how my sons and grandsons betrayed me; I would have passed it on to you. It is land, a piece of Albania, an estate, a farm, call it what you like: it is still land, earth. But the Albanians would not yield. It's too late, they would say. And they did not even have much sympathy for his age. On the contrary, it infuriated them more than anything. He might moan like four hundred old beggars. His senescence merely showed that he had delayed. Nobody would excuse him his negligence. It was unforgivable to forget Albania for forty days, let alone forty years. Now that circumstances had forced him to remember her, it was too late. He had long been deaf towards her, and now she, too, was deaf to him.

How fickle my Albania has been, he thought, staring with bemusement at the distant wintry mountains as if for the first time. How long had he felt like this? He delved deep into his mind. Had he really not loved her? Had he thought only of himself, had he neglected her? But what other land could I love more than her, he exclaimed to himself. Wallachia? Greece? Bosnia? I did everything for Albania, even if I sometimes despaired of her, and who could say that I loved another country more? But at the very moment when he thought that he had silenced these invisible critics (for indeed most of his opponents were in prisons or buried under the earth, though the wind still carried their damned griping), a small voice inside him said: Ali, nobody says you didn't love Albania, because you're an Albanian too, but you didn't love her enough. And in your case not loving her enough is the same as not loving her at all. Albania might have accepted someone else's casual attentions, but not yours, because she expected a lot from you. His head sank into his beard in a gesture of recognition. Albania did not want just any kind of love. The love she demanded was special, self-effacing, urgent, aching, a love to the death.

He tried to distract his exhausted mind, but a gnawing doubt remained. Had the Fourth Directorate discovered Albania's deafness to his appeal? He would tell Vasiliqia that of course it had, because the sultan's letters were becoming increasingly frosty. Now the salutations at the end, those brilliant peacock's feathers, were omitted entirely.

The Fourth Directorate, he muttered to himself. He had despised it for so many years and made fun of it, while quietly it had continued its work. For years, it had been aware of his silent rebellion against the Sublime Porte. He had slipped out of the sovereign's hands like crumbling soil. His disobedience and even mockery were clearly legible between the polite phrases of his correspondence. He had held talks with the British and with Bonaparte without informing his Padishah at all. He had invited or expelled consuls at whim, and had turned up at great battles with his own army or not, as it suited him. All these facts were well known and discussed openly in high circles, but still the sultan had turned a blind eye. *He's scared of crossing me,* Ali Pasha used to boast. Ali enjoyed playing with fire, because this more than anything else gave him a sense of power. Without this game, the last years of his life would have been dull. With every passing day, he more obviously baited the sultan. The sultan often sent him invitations to feasts, but he declined these with derision. He knew what to expect at one of those magnificent dinners: poison in his food, and then, the next day, his head in the Traitor's Niche.

Weeks passed, couriers returned from the capital, and it was now evident to everyone that the sultan was fearful of making their rift known. Every week the Fourth Directorate filed copies of reports sent by foreign ambassadors to their governments, informing them that the sultan's writ counted for nothing in Albania. It was not only the salons, but all kinds of military and even clerical circles that talked openly about the quarrel, in anger or with scorn. Several times the censor was forced to ban the daily newspapers because of poisonous barbs aimed indirectly at the government's apathy. How long would the capital tolerate the situation?

Undercover agents prowled the Albanian lands. Their activities were reported in detail to Ali Pasha, who split his sides with mirth. *What else will they find? Isn't it obvious that I no longer obey the Sublime Porte? What else can they* look for? These men in the ministries of the capital seem real blockheads. Let them find out all they want about my mischief, he told his loyal followers. Let my Padishah drink this bitter cup to the dregs.

Ali Pasha did not realize that this same Fourth Directorate, which he had scorned all his life, was digging his grave. It was only in recent months, as his downfall drew near, that he had come to understand what these agents were after as they stalked the land dressed as tramps or gypsies from remote parts of the province. His own insubordination was of no interest to them. They spent their days and nights gauging the possible reaction of the population, if it came to an armed conflict with the capital. And when in the end the work was done, the material gathered and scrutinized, and all possible alternatives assessed (as he learned later from his own spies), there came that terrible letter from the Padishah, like a thunderclap out of a blue sky. "I will turn you to ash, ash, ash," the emperor wrote. The suddenly outlawed pasha turned this letter over in his hands, reflecting on the sound of this word, *ash*, which resembled a gust of the sultan's laughter, or a snake that slithered towards him from the expanses of Asia, to coil itself around his throat.

Their confrontation was at last out in the open. But it was not its publication that so shocked Ali Pasha, who was rarely shocked, but something else: the discovery that the sultan had delayed his fight with him for so long not because he was afraid of him, but out of "fear of a repetition of unpleasant history." That was what was written in the Fourth Directorate's final report, which Ali's spies had managed to lay their hands on. Wounding words followed: "This possibility, in our view, can now be discounted. Albania will not follow Black Ali as it followed the apostate Scanderbeg."

So the sultan had issued his declaration of war as soon as it was diagnosed that Albania would leave the old vizier to face his imperial fury alone.

Ali stared out at the wintry plains for hours. The occasional bird flew over them, looking like a military crest, and, as if to persuade himself that what he saw was real, he muttered under his breath, "So this is Albania. *Shqi-për-i-a.*" He pronounced its name in the Albanian language, dividing it into four syllables. This name sounded alien. He was used to the Ottoman name, Arnautistan, which had always seemed to him more natural. Now he understood why. It made him feel safe, because with this name the country seemed to belong to him, while this other one, which belonged half to this earth and half to heaven, somehow scared him. "*Shqipëria,*" he repeated slowly, like a toddler pronouncing for the first time *mother* or *father*. It had taken him until the age of eighty to stammer the name of the land that had given him birth. It is too late for me, he almost cried aloud. It was too late for everything. Darkness had fallen all around him. He was, after all, called Black Ali. Ali of the night.

Sunk in these thoughts, he sat numb and inert for the first few days after his pronouncement as a traitor. Then he slowly came to life again and sent his messengers in all directions to issue another call to arms. But its echo faded and dissolved into the air. Nobody replied except a few crazy old men from a distant province, who, they said, turned up because they were spoiling for a fight of the kind they missed. As soon as they'd had enough—after three or four days, no more—they would go home again.

The decree proclaiming Black Ali's treason had no doubt been dispatched already, and that repulsive crawler from the court, the one who colored his hair with henna like a woman, would arrive in maybe three or four days. Then, a week later at most, the army would begin its march. For some reason, Ali began explaining to Vasiliqia the tiniest details of how a royal army left to crush a rebellion.

At its head, in front even of the banners and crests, infantrymen carried huge scarecrows on their shoulders. "Scarecrows?" she asked in amazement and horror. "Effigies? Why?" She imagined hundreds of scarecrows in the frozen fields, swaying stiffly in the wind, and her skin crept.

"Why scarecrows?" she murmured, shuddering from an uncanny horror provoked not by the dark or any fearful sights but merely by a pale light across a plain. She looked away with downcast eyes and wondered why it was that everything connected to her husband's fate was so unnatural. Things appeared strangely transfigured, immobilized as if at the touch of a thousand witches and warlocks at once, when he talked about Albania. She tried hard to align her own experience of the country with the one he talked about, but she sensed immediately that her Albania was different from his. For Vasiliqia, Albania was quite tangible, with its plateaus and grazing lands rimed with frost, with morning sleep broken by the rhythm of the plunger in the milk churn, impatient hours filled with embroidery for her dowry, patches of sun by the church, and the call of the cuckoo. But for her husband it was different: a country frozen as if in a trance, above which the moon and the stars were mere state emblems and crests, horribly lifeless like scarecrows. She had seen scarecrows in the wheat fields with birds circling nearby. But when he talked about scarecrows they were different: they moved through empty space with no wheat or birds, only the winter wind blowing through their rags.

"But why scarecrows?" she asked for the third time. He pried open his jaw more to grimace than to speak, as he always did when asked to make annoying explanations. He told her that the scarecrows were to show contempt for the enemy, or in this case the rebels. So they represented in a way his premature dethronement. "But the sultan doesn't know," he snarled, "that when my day comes I will march on his capital not with a couple of hundred scarecrows, but with a thousand, forty thousand . . ."

She tried to put the scarecrows out of her mind, but they kept reappearing at the edge of her vision, slowly, coldly drifting towards her as if sliding on snow.

Meanwhile, Ali Pasha waited in the southern tower for his spies to return from the capital city with their road dust and news. First of all he wanted to know who'd be commanding the campaign against him. When a spy brought a reliable report that the counterinsurgency forces would be led by

Bugrahan, a third-rank pasha, Ali astonished the informer, who thought this news would delight his master, by raising his hands to his head as if this were a calamity.

Ali had expected someone else: the Padishah himself, or at least the grand vizier. The threat to him had to be as impressive as possible, the army the biggest, the artillery the most frightening: everything on a huge scale, as befitted an imperial campaign. These things did not scare him. What was important was that he was shown respect. So this news broke his spirit. Two sultans in succession had gone forth against Scanderbeg, and what sultans—Murad the Great and Mehmed the Conqueror. Now this ninny from the military academy, someone he had not even deigned to look upon at state ceremonies, had been chosen to fight him.

Anger jolted him out of his lassitude. He calmed down a little, recalling that even against Scanderbeg the campaign had been launched by less distinguished pashas, before the grand viziers and the sultans themselves took up arms in turn. You will come, you will all come, he muttered to himself. In turn, according to rank, as in court protocol . . . and then in turn the crows will caw over you.

His messengers and couriers departed again for all parts of Albania. Ali nurtured a hope that now that he had mended his ways, his country might forgive him. Perhaps Albania would take pity on his advanced years and howling loneliness, which was like the solitude of an aged thunderbolt with barely the strength to crack the sky. But again no response came. His hard-hearted country forgave him nothing. The first courier came back with nothing, as did the second, and the third, the fourth, the sixth, the eleventh. "What is wrong with my country?" he grumbled under his breath. Even now, when the forces against him were on their way, the Albanians made no move. Even Greece was taking up arms, he thought despondently. A foreign country was taking advantage of his quarrel with the sultan. The Greeks, thought Vasiliqia, are profiting precisely because they are foreign to you and you are foreign to them. That is why they are profiting. In the last six months, Vasiliqia had learned more about the state than the students of the Royal Institute did in ten years. She understood that the Greeks, who had hated Ali Pasha all his life, were now making use of him, and would cast him aside when the right time came. For the Greeks, he was like a treasure found by the side of the road that nobody had missed. Albania would never have treated him like that.

Ali had come to accept that Albania would leave him to his fate. He had sworn never to abandon this old crone of a country: the two would go down together, leaving a chaos behind them, like a primordial dust. Now he realized that he would fall by himself. She would remain aboveground, and the rains would fall on her as always, the almonds would blossom in April, and the bleating of the sheep and the leaves of the maize stalks would be the same. Her emblems alone might perhaps change . . . The thought of this abandonment made him want to howl.

No, Albania will always remember me, he groaned to

himself. It will remember me when I am gone, but it will be too late.

His imagination was so goaded by anger and weighed down by misery that he could no longer think straight. His legend was already taking shape. He knew that he would be remembered, but whether as good or bad, he couldn't tell.

His thoughts ran off in all directions like feral cats, but never towards the future. What lay before him was covered by mists and there were precipices on whose brink he had always paused, and turned back dazed. Now he stood for the first time looking out over this ocean, dumbfounded and mercilessly oppressed by its vastness.

He sat stunned for days on end and Vasiliqia sometimes thought that his gray beard had grown over his mouth and he would never speak again. His insensibility was frightening. Then he came to himself again, overcoming what resembled a frozen wasteland of cloud around him. From deep inside himself, he drew up as if from a well something precious that he had perhaps been keeping for evil days: his own death. This is what he would launch at future generations like some cursed cannonball. "I have you and I have death," he said to Vasiliqia as soon as his mind cleared.

The plans for his own death absorbed him for whole days, while the punitive armies of Bugrahan Pasha encircled the castle.

At first these plans were informed by his envy of Scanderbeg, who had had a quarter-century of glorious rebellion behind him but died an ordinary death in his bed, of a common fever, with wet cloths on his brow and his wife sitting dimly by his head. Ali would not end like that.

He dragged himself out of the past and stared into the future. He was caught between the past and future, like between two mountains. Ali Pasha the outlaw, without a state, without Albania, confronting a gray abyss in which gales blew the ravens now in one direction and now in another. The thundering vizier. But was this abyss slightly less impressive than the mountains? He thought for a moment. With his death he would ignite over this abyss a great shooting star.

Not long ago the news had arrived of the death of his friend Napoleon Bonaparte, the little pasha of France, as they called him in these parts. His death, too, had been muted. He had died in bed like an old lady of Tepelena and, moreover, as a prisoner. At about this time they brought him a new book by that English lord with the limp who had been a guest in his castle. The book was called *Childe Harold's Pilgrimage* and in one part the Englishman wrote about Ali Pasha. One of Ali's scribes read it to him. He listened in silence and then took the book in his hands, looking carefully at the little letters, those crafty ants that were supposed to carry his name on their wretched backs for centuries to come. He threw the book aside. If that was immortality, he spat in its face. He didn't need books to be remembered. Haxhi Sherreti told him once that the king of Persia had ordered a poet, a certain Ferdowsi, to write a great poem, paying a gold piece for every line. Other kings built pyramids, mosques, temples, mausoleums, and shrines to their own posthumous glory. Ali didn't need pillars and domes. He would plan his own monument. Aged, besieged, and abandoned by everybody, in the few days and nights left to him he would sketch the architecture of his own death.

All pyramids and monuments, however magnificent, crumbled under the sun and wind, but death, with its interiors, gloomy cupolas, frescoes, portals, and perspectives of no return, was a structure that nothing could erode. And so he would project his death into the future. Would any other tomb rival his?

Intoxicated by this idea, he began to work out the plan. He ignored the nuances and drew a bold line through the gray nothingness of the sky, or let a cataract fall from the middle of the heavens, over there . . . He knew that from now on he had nothing that might be called a life. What he was now experiencing was more like death than life. It tasted different, and finer, like all rare things. Sometimes it occurred to him that he was suffering from a delusion, what his soldiers from the north would call the work of sprites. But he quickly banished that chill thought.

It was while he was under this fever, and after a long and inexplicable delay, that the decree arrived proclaiming him a traitor to religion and the state. The courier with the hennaed beard came before him. Ali's chief retainers and Vasiliqia were present. They waited for him to say or do something. But Ali faltered. He had anticipated this blow, but still his heart failed him. He cursed himself for a chicken-livered coward. What else had he expected? Finally, with trembling hands, he unwrapped the decree. His eyes were not reading the contents, which he had predicted long ago, but were fixed somewhere remote. Placing the document on the table so that the sultan's script was plain to see, he folded four fingers into a fist and pressed his thumbnail into the imperial signature in the universal gesture of a man crushing an insect. Everybody around stood motionless.

This was his last grand gesture. Other days came, without gestures but full of everyday cares. In the first week, inspired by fresh enthusiasm, he inflicted two serious defeats on Bugrahan Pasha. The following week it was learned that Bugrahan Pasha had been dismissed and his head was being carried post-haste to the capital city, to be lodged in the Traitor's Niche.

Ali climbed the highest tower with Vasiliqia and pointed out to her the road on which couriers took important messages or severed heads to the capital. "They dream of carrying my head on that road," he said, and laughed. From the castle walls they could see the besieging army's multitude of tents. Among them, through his long spyglass, Ali sought the tent of the newly appointed commander-in-chief, the army's rising star. For the last six months it had been whispered he would become prime minister.

During all those days, while the thirty thousand soldiers of Hurshid Pasha clashed with his two regiments of guards, the Tosk guards from the south and the Gheg guards from the north, Ali dedicated himself to the cult of his own death. He planned it out by himself, far from anybody, and nobody, not even Vasiliqia herself, knew what it would be like, only that it would be glorious . . . Ali had mumbled something about barrels of gunpowder, which at the last moment would blow up the castle and everything in it. The flames would rise to heaven, and the molten gold of his treasure, his pearls and bloody rubies, would fall on all sides, as if from a coronet of hell.

Make your ablutions. Whenever Vasiliqia thought of his glorious death, these terrible words flooded her mind, a chill torrent that threatened to sweep away his carefully constructed memorial. It was the phrase pronounced to a condemned man just before his beheading: "Make your ablutions and prepare for death."

Since his death, in this first week in a world without him, these words had stuck in Vasiliqia's mind. She wandered through the countless chambers of the castle and in every corner imagined a voice whispering to her: "Make your ablutions."

There was a rumor that after the *katil ferman*, which declared her husband a traitor, another decree had arrived, pardoning him. The drums in the Turkish camp, announcing the arrival of the *hayir ferman*, the Decree of Clemency, could be heard in the deepest recesses of the castle. Ali's spies in the enemy camp reported seeing this decree with their own eyes when Hurshid Pasha himself had unrolled it in front of all the nobles. Ali summoned Vasiliqia to his rooms. "Listen," he said, "I had prepared for a great death, not for my own sake, because our deaths do not belong to ourselves alone, but for yours. Now the sultan is pardoning me. Why should you deserve this pretty spectacle?" This was the first time that she had heard him talk with such disdain. "I will go as governor to some dull province, where there's nothing to worry about, and no glory. The empire is vast, and they tell me there are provinces where nothing has happened for a hundred years. I'll be sent somewhere like that."

She listened to him, wide-eyed. As she stared, the mountain crumbled abruptly, like in a nightmare, and the thunderclaps turned into faint tinkles . . . What a wicked wife I am to him, she thought. He is eighty-two years old, white-haired. He makes the entire empire tremble, and this isn't enough for me. Do I want him dead too? What a wicked wife.

"Why are you looking at me like that?" he said to her. "If the order is false, which I think it might be, then you'll see what I will do."

Perhaps she was the first to realize that the decree was a trick. The couriers bearing it approached with an unnatural gait, as if on wooden legs, and their faces were pale.

"Wait there," he called to them when they were twenty paces off. "What is your news?"

The courier raised high the decree in his hand.

"Death, Ali. Make your ablutions and . . ."

Gunfire blazed on both sides and all was confusion. Amid the mayhem she saw someone drag Ali down the stairs. Her eyes were still wide. "Now you see his death," said a gentle voice by her temple. There it is: seven wooden stairs and the sound of a head hitting them . . . and then, a moment before she lost consciousness, she saw the scarecrows advancing with their stiff movements across the wintry plain. "No," she screamed, "not them . . ." and fell to the ground.

Ali's widow led her entourage out into the clean air high at the top of the northern tower. She went to the parapet and gazed at the icy continental waste that stretched beyond the open plain. Perhaps because of its endlessness, this wide expanse, above which blackbirds flew, brought to mind her own loneliness.

In the midst of this solitude a carriage drawn by horses with manes cut in mourning had stopped by the roadside. The carriage was ready for a journey and stood waiting for Ali's widow. So often her husband had promised to take her to the capital city for the royal celebrations, but he had never done so. Now she was going there by herself.

She was alone in the world, in February.

The desolate highway connecting two continents lay before her. The previous week, his head had set off along it. His body had been buried here, and as she'd walked with bowed head at the front of the funeral cortege, her mind had revolved around a single thought seemingly pinned down by a nail: that she was accompanying only one half of her husband to the grave, and indeed that half which had been totally alien to her.

She had hardly got to know his body in their rare marital relations. It had never occurred to her before, but when she heard that his head had departed, it struck her that, for her, this man had existed only from the neck up. The other part of him was merely a gorgeous robe, with the insignia of a ruler embroidered on it, and nothing else.

She went on staring at the plain and her two escorts glanced at each other, as if to say, will we have to look for treasure in the fields, too?

Nothing had been clear to her when Ali's relationship with the sultan had begun to cool. She looked at this broad landscape filled with cottages, trees trembling in the wind, haystacks and barns, like every plain in the world, and imagined it shaken and stripped of all these things, and filled with secrets, horsemen in the night, and mysterious dervishes and monks. It was as if the land were giving birth to ghosts conceived long ago.

Now that nightmare was over, the plain had become a plain again. The carriage with its horses with trimmed manes stood waiting and she, the widow of Ali Pasha the Black, was setting off across that flatland, on the road that had brought the winds of his final autumn, the couriers, the letters, and in the end the scarecrows.

She was still surrounded by her solitude. The carriage would leave and then she would slowly enter the continent of grief. All that space would close in on her and her loneliness would be spread in a thin layer across the immensity of Eurasia.

6

Still on the Frontier

FROST MUST have settled on the great tent in the night, to judge by the cracking sounds of the canvas in the blustering wind. They sat or half reclined on camp beds, most blowing on their cold hands and cursing the fumes from the stove, which the gale sent back inside. Some pulled at pipes and brooded, tapping the ash onto the mats and watching the curling smoke in surprise. Two were playing chess, a couple were reading, and a few others in the corner next to the stove listened to the Jew Elias, who was telling a story. A soldier came and went, bringing coffee and removing empty cups.

"Soldier, bring me more coffee. There's no way I can sleep at night anyway," said a slight man with a brittle, glassy sheen to his thin face.

They had arrived three days ago, and still couldn't start their duties as a special unit sent from headquarters should, but were spending many idle hours recalling incidents that had happened on other missions of this sort, making comparisons and jokes and complaining about shortcomings of every kind, as administrators from central offices usually do when they go on missions to the back of beyond.

Lala Shahini entered, with a sour expression in total contrast to the cheerful curls falling over his brow.

"What's going on outside?" someone asked from the corner, without raising his head.

"Nothing. Cold. Wind . . . soughing . . . is that what you call the wind off the lake in your parts? I saw that swine with a bell, the pronouncer of curses."

"And what was that scumbag doing?" asked the first voice.

Lala Shahini pursed his lips and grimaced in disdain.

"It drives me wild to see bastards like that," he said. "They make my blood boil. A character like that comes out, curses the fortress at the start of the war, a job done in the blink of an eye, and draws a salary for an entire year."

"Hehe," laughed Elias the Jew. "Why get upset, Lala? Cursing obstacles in the path of the glorious troops is one of the oldest army regulations. An army can do without a cook, but a curse-giver? No way."

The glassy-faced man's laugh resembled the tinkling of glasses. His cheeks and forehead shook and then his face went rigid.

"Do you know," someone butted in, "another group's coming soon from headquarters, to survey Ali Tepelena's estate."

"And what will happen to this estate?"

They went on to talk about the dead pasha's lands.

"Are the news-criers still reading the decree?" asked one of the chess players.

Lala Shahini nodded.

The other man swore under his breath.

"The decree alone is enough to crush all hope, never mind the curse-giver. Moldy decrees copied by doddery old codgers who don't know where Albania is. In this case, better not to send units like ours at all."

"There's no way the decrees can be specific if there's been no decision about Albania yet," Lala Shahini said.

For a while they speculated about the expected decree. In the last four hundred years, Albania's status had fluctuated many times: low, abysmal, medium, high, low again, then sort of high and low, and so on. Precedents could be found for anything that happened, and just as well for anything that didn't happen.

"Then why did they send us so urgently, and in the middle of winter?" whined the glassy-faced man.

They'd asked this question many times since that bitterly cold morning when they received the order to leave at once for Albania. Oh God, why this hurry? they had wondered as they bade farewell to their appalled wives at the gates of their houses, as they collected their mission documents, and finally, on the endless road leading to the Balkans. The process of stripping a land of its national identity—Caw-caw as it was called—took a century, and there could be no reason to hurry.

"Seriously, why did they send us out so quickly?" somebody said, echoing the thin man.

"Perhaps to placate the party that wants revenge on Albania," said Elias the Jew. "Do you remember the commotion in the newspapers when we left? Do you remember the headlines? 'The Ravens Leave for Albania' . . . 'Albania's Erasure Begins' . . . 'Albania—Year Zero.'"

"It might be as Elias says," someone spoke up. "We've probably come for no reason, just to give them a fright. Like that scarecrow business."

"That means neither bloodshed nor Caw-caw," Lala Shahini said. "So what other consequence is there?"

"There's only one status that Albania hasn't been through, as far as I know," one man said. "Or only for a short time. A state of emergency."

"Ouch," went Lala Shahini, hunching his shoulders.

"They've been relying on that more and more often recently."

They recalled situations and provinces in which a "state of emergency" had been imposed. In archaic language, these provinces were called lieux of strife or loci of conflict, which the consuls usually translated as "trouble spots." A "state of emergency" would be devised by the First Directorate of the Interior Ministry to stimulate internal divisions on the basis of religion, regional and feudal allegiances, castes, and traditions. The experts responsible for this collaborated with the Central Archive, exploiting its documentation.

"We once traveled through a province of that kind," Lala Shahini said, "and I'll never forget it as long as I live."

The slight, glassy-faced man listened to them abstractedly. His mind was elsewhere. He thought that in both cases, if Albania were declared a "cursed land" or ended up as a "trouble spot," the result would be the same. In the first case, the army would take control and the specialists in repression would come with their files, rulebooks, and toolkits. They would open all the old chronicles of terrible slaughter, which recorded all the tortures that had ever been inflicted on the human race anywhere in the world: crucifixion, impalement on stakes, the smashing of bones, sawing in two, burial alive, tearing apart with horses, crushing by camels, skinning alive, roasting in ovens, boiling in cauldrons, and so on. All these things would happen here, while they, the staff of the Central Archive, would be far away, over there. As far away as possible, he thought. It was several days' journey to the capital city, with its daily working routine, its frosty mornings when thousands of civil servants hurried to their desks to keep to the official working day, the long hours hunched over files, numb hands, failing eyesight. Yet, as spring drew closer, the days would be clearer and warmer, and besides, in spring he was getting married.

His friends teased him about it. He was an expert in wedding customs, funeral rites, and different traditions—work that was considered of secondary importance compared with the main fields such as the ideology of rebellion, which was the preserve of the team leader, and national mentality, which was Elias the Jew's subject. National memory was Lala Shahini's speciality, and language belonged to the Mute, the oldest among them, whose real name was long forgotten. But still there were occasions when wedding customs counted for something. Although they teased him about it, they knew that if the terrible decision of Caw-caw were taken, and a country was to be stripped of its national identity, then he, like the others, would be ready to organize, with figures and precise deadlines, all the possible ways to debase, distort, or eliminate entirely the wedding rites of the newly subjugated people. This was considered an important matter in the capital city because research had shown long ago that weddings had been the origin of theater, one of the most diabolical of Christian inventions. Teasing him about his protracted bachelorhood, they often said to him, "It'll be a strange day when you get married, Harun, after all the weddings you've ruined." He laughed in his special way and said to himself, it really will be a strange day. In their big house in the capital city, his many aunts and uncles frequently talked about his future wedding. Although these conversations were cheerful, he felt that their good spirits sometimes concealed a small element of sorrow, like a shard of glass. He had been the only child, always delicate, and the darling of a great household whose official connections went back many generations. It was a disappointment to the whole family when, instead of choosing a religious or diplomatic career, he had preferred to become a staff member of the Central Archive. Even now, after so many years, they mentioned his choice with bitterness, while he chuckled to himself and knew they would never understand what extraordinary expertise his job involved.

Whenever in his research he discovered ancient decrees mentioning royal titles, such as the glorious Padishah Selim the Grim, scion of scions of sultans, king of kings, emperor above emperors until the day of doom, conqueror of territories beyond measurement and augmenter of the lands of Islam, subjugator of two empires, conqueror of eight kingdoms, destroyer of three hundred cities, king of the Arabs, Persians, and Rumelians, etc., etc., he would automatically think of himself: Harun Ibra, diminisher of happiness on this earth, who turns brides pale, dulls the glitter of their dowries, and withers their sex, the shrinker of testicles, spoiler of a billion weddings until the day of doom. Sometimes this thought horrified him. He tried to put it out of his mind, but even when he succeeded, he still baulked at the idea that his own wedding was imminent. Soon, next spring, perhaps in autumn, his wedding day would come . . . and then . . . what then? An obscure fear of retribution fluttered deep inside him. For as old people said, disrupting a wedding is worse than destroying a bridge. But he quickly reassured himself. After all, these were the weddings of rebels. Harun Ibra had spoiled the joy of Albanians, Hungarians, Greeks, Serbs, Jews, Bulgarians, Czechs, Poles, Macedonians, Croats, Armenians, Georgians, Azerbaijanis, Montenegrins, Palestinians, Egyptians, Lebanese, Uzbeks, Kyrgyz, Moldovans, and Romanians. And besides, this was a slow massacre, the protracted grief of centuries. It was a cinch compared with the work of experts in ruthlessness, who, for research purposes, spent hours on end by cauldrons in which people boiled, or scaffolds where rebels were skinned.

Around him they were still talking about Albania.

"Yes, yes, you're right," the Mute was saying to Elias the Jew. "It won't be stripped of its nationality, or put to the sword. Caw-caw is a thing of the past, and it's impossible to use force in a country that has filled nearly a quarter of the empire's high offices. The Albanians have served the state faithfully for years. None of them want to see their country soaked in blood."

"You think a trouble spot doesn't involve bloodshed?" Lala Shahini asked.

"Oh, that's different," said Elias the Jew. "In that case, they themselves will be at one another's throats. That's something else."

"And besides, in Albania, like in all the Balkans, imposing a state of emergency would suit the nature of the people, wouldn't it, Elias?" the Mute said.

The Jew nodded.

"A friend of mine who works in the First Directorate told me it had been a superhuman task a few years ago to impose a state of emergency in a northern province, somewhere beyond Romania," Elias said. "It was impossible. They were such a gentle people. Nothing would provoke them . . . so they decided to obliterate the entire nation instead."

"But in the Balkans it's different," Lala Shahini said. He

touched his leather bag with his thumb. "In here, I've got all the quarrels among Albanian nobles from the time of Scanderbeg to the present day."

The others stared at this hitherto unnoticed bag.

"No end of squabbling," he went on. "About property, women, the vacant throne, ill-advised jokes, dogs, hunting falcons, and the devil knows what."

As he spoke, he rubbed the bag with his hand, as if its leather would yield the facts he needed.

One of the tasks of the section in which Lala worked was to trace the genealogies of the families, most now extinct, of Albanian leaders. This work had been going on for centuries. The fear that some surviving progeny might revive the famous name of a dead nobleman made a nightmare of the lives of the entire staff, from the director down to ordinary clerks. They knew that if such a thing happened, they would bear the brunt of the official fury, and so, to avert such a catastrophe, they watched with perpetual vigilance. By day they kept their quarry under constant surveillance, and by night they shouted in fitful sleep. Their files contained everything about the great Albanian families—their origins, their marriage ties, and their enmities—in a complete chronicle that followed them until they were extinguished. After the episode of Scanderbeg, in which they had all taken part and shared in its stellar glory, the nobles had fled from the conquered country. They had scattered like ravens throughout Europe, and eventually died out. First the Balshajs became extinct in the fifteenth century, even before their lands were occupied. The Kastriots melted away a century later, in Rome. The Muzakajs died out in about 1600, and the Aranits at the same time. The Dukagjins disappeared in the vicinity of Venice in the seventeenth century, and the rest no one knew where.

Lala Shahini heard the other men's voices as if from a distance. Whenever the old leaders of Albania were mentioned, his spirits drooped a little.

Having pored over their stories for so many years, Lala Shahini had slowly, unwittingly, started to feel fond of these aristocrats. And so, whenever the conversation turned to them, he fell silent, so as not to betray himself. In fact, he was enthralled. Their names, a little mangled in his friends' pronunciation, floated like scraps of cloud under the canopy of the winter tent.

He had followed them year by year and century by century from the time when some of them, partly under pressure, but more wooed by Ottoman flattery, made small concessions. First they altered their calendar, and then changed their titles of count and duke to pasha and vizier. Sometimes in despair, but more often cheerfully and ironically, the men donned turbans and the women veils, as if they were costumes that might be set aside when the feast was over. And so they connived in their own extinction.

When they had come to their senses and genuinely wanted to put off these disguises, they found it was not so easy. At the same time they would lose their reputations or even their heads. In fury, and led by Scanderbeg of the Kastriots, they then rose in a terrible rebellion that lasted almost forty years.

Lala Shahini had traced the defeat of each one of them, and the subsequent flight to Europe of the survivors. Some entered the service of foreign kings and fought in other wars, winning promotion and honors, but these wars were of a different, tepid kind, as was the glory they won.

Despite the Central Archive's strenuous efforts to erase these nobles from the face of the earth, their names remained scattered throughout the terrain of Albania. These reckless, impetuous, stubborn people were transformed into valleys, crags, plains, copses, and waterfalls. The lands of Balshikia, Karlilija, Shpati, the streams of Skuria, Myzeqeja, the Plain of Dukagjin, Mount Scanderbeg. After so many centuries, they still loomed among the mists in motionless stone, immured, untouched by the perpetual fever of struggles for power, of quarrels and spite.

Lala Shahini listened to the conversation and gathered that it had moved on from the nobles of the past to those of today. The discussion, like some great dish of pilaf, drew everyone together. People talked in pairs or threes, and their exchanges leaped easily across one another. They mentioned these lords and ladies one by one and compared them first to one another and then to their ancestors. "The Greeks have no reason to curse Ali Tepelena in their songs," said one man. "They profited from him, and now they've got the bit between their teeth." "That's how stepchildren always behave," replied Elias the Jew. "Always ungrateful." "The Albanians won't be spoiled anymore," said the Mute again.

This phrase was being repeated millions of times in every corner of the vast empire, Lala Shahini thought, just like after the fall of Albania centuries before. At that time, decrees had come one after another like thunder in April, but each one was milder than the last until, like lightning in a clear sky, there arrived the Decree of Reconciliation, which began with the words "Albania is my joy." Then, not only were dozens of pashas of the land and sea decorated in the same year, to show that this policy was not going to change again, but Albanians were made prime ministers of the entire empire, not for appearances' sake, but for almost a century.

Whenever Lala Shahini remembered the Qyprili family, he would smile to himself and shake his head in admiration. The sultan wears the crown, but the Qyprilis steer the helm of state, everybody said of them, the only family in the world to inherit the post of grand vizier, like a dynasty. Browsing through the files of the Archive, Lala Shahini had unearthed hundreds of letters from senior functionaries, clergy, wizards, prophets, imams, and ordinary dervishes, all addressed to sultans, in which they begged the emperors to change this perverse policy of inheritance, warning them and even threatening them with the prospect of divine revenge if they did not. The letters had come from all parts, written in every kind of alphabet, in living and dead languages. Sometimes they were accompanied by mysterious symbols, or beards cut as a sign of grief at this calamity, or doctors' certificates testifying that worry over this matter had deprived the writer of his sleep or had caused blindness, deafness, asthma, jaundice, melting of the innards like candle wax, swelling of the knees, scrofula, constriction of the neck, and so forth. There were letters written in blood, as was to be expected, but the most shocking of all was a short message sent in a state of extreme desperation with the severed hand of the writer. When even this missive had no effect, it was understood that no human entreaty or agency could redress this wrong, and the only hope lay in divine intervention.

Lala Shahini stifled a sigh. The hand of God had struck at last, and with a heavy blow. Yet an inner voice told him that Albania would not be undone this time either. On the road to Janina, as the storm of malice and vindictiveness against Ali Tepelena broke, he had tried to console himself with the thought that the Albanian nobles of today were totally unlike those of the past, and there was no need to worry so much about them. Of course, they were similar in their furious, foaming rages, but at the first serious setback they would change their turban-clad minds. An Asiatic obscurity, like the stifling steam of a bathhouse that distorts and conceals many things, distanced them from the nobles of the past—remote, alpine, snow-covered, blue-misted, wrapped always in a great cloud of nostalgia—the Balshajs, Topiajs, Dukagjins, Muzakajs, and Kastriots. Or so he told himself, but a nagging worry remained. He felt that the world needed folly of this kind: life would be duller without it, and secretly he prayed that these nobles would survive.

The discussion around him continued as lively as ever, but the expressions of hope gradually diminished. Now they were talking again about the files and the surprises they contained.

They were prepared for anything. Before leaving the capital, they had spent day after day in the reading rooms of the Archive, bent over the thousand files about Albania. These files recorded everything about the country: the cities, villages, heights of the bell towers, rivers, standing waters, castles, swamps, secret sects, graveyards, bridges, water mills, fairy tales, windblown sandbanks, earthquakes, regional dialects, embroidery, avalanches, weddings, laments, genealogies, clans, kinship groups large and small, churches, monasteries, the coldness of the sea, households and families counted by their hearths or chimneys or their maternal origin, the heads of tribes, known as the chiefs of the mountains, the blood feuds, alliances in marriage, patriarchs, inherited diseases, antique theaters, spies, oceans, and so forth.

There were many other halls, every one spacious and cold, with high windows pierced by a light that bore little relation to the season outside and was always gray and chill, as if straight from regions where the weather never changed. The Archive's staff had toiled throughout December. The massive building was never heated because of the danger of fire, and the workers had suffered greatly from the cold. Everything was icy: the tables, the files, and their own fingers, which turned to lead on the pages. No fire was lit in the central hall either: the Top Hall, as it was called because of its height.

Only the senior staff worked there, and section heads were rarely summoned. The director of Caw-caw worked there, or the Big Raven, as the staff called him among themselves. It was said that the emperor himself received him at a special meeting every three months, but nobody knew when or why.

The partial or full erasure of the national identity of peoples, which was the main task of the Central Archive, was carried out according to the old secret doctrine of Caw-caw and passed through five principal stages: first, the physical crushing of rebellion; second, the extirpation of any idea of rebellion; third, the destruction of culture, art, and tradition; fourth, the eradication or impoverishment of the language; and fifth, the extinction or enfeeblement of the national memory.

The briefest of all these stages was the physical crushing of rebellion, which merely meant war, but the longest phase was the reduction of the language into Nonspeak, as it was called for short.

The files on dead languages were stored on a heavy bronze shelf. These files were thick, and most of their pages had been wiped clean with the greatest care. Words had been expunged from dictionaries, rules of grammar and syntax had gradually been erased until they vanished from use, and finally the letters of the alphabet were rubbed out. This was the final spasm of the written language, after which its death was certified. Then began the longer and more laborious task of eradicating the spoken language. This also had its intermediate stages. The final phase was the extinction of the language in its last outposts: old women. It had been shown that, in general, languages survived longer among women, and especially among women who had borne children. Finally, when the language had been wiped from the face of the earth, there came a time when the old women, too, died out: like ancient goddesses, they preserved the last ashen remnants of the spoken tongue. They were recorded in special notebooks as "aged female speakers" and were under constant surveillance until they died. After this, the extinction of the language and its transformation into Nonspeak was considered complete.

Centuries of experience was stored in the files of the Archive: schedules for the extinction of languages, their unexpected rallies and their last gasps—in short, everything except the vanished languages themselves. The thousands of pages of files did not contain a single trace of them, not a word, not a syllable. Their total extermination was carried out with the intention of precluding any revival.

For a long time, there had been conflicting views on whether to preserve the corpses of these languages. Some said that at least one file in the Archive should conserve them in mummified form, but others insisted that this served no purpose and could lead dangerously to their resurrection. The second view held sway in the end. Its supporters had found in old chronicles the case of the revival of a language, which the chroniclers had called in horror a "Christ among languages." Nobody knew, they wrote, how a long-dead language could appear once again on the surface of the earth.

People discovered speaking it were hunted down as they fled through the marshlands, clamped in irons, and cut up, but still these victims would not or could not say where they had found this forbidden language. Long investigations were conducted in the Archive, and the list of officials who had worked in the Top Hall was checked name by name against their entrances and exits, but without any conclusion. The matter remained a mystery to historians, who lost their sleep and peace of mind. "This thing remains inexplicable," the chroniclers wrote, and their skin crept with horror.

With these pages from the chronicle in their hands, the hard-liners easily won.

However, the files on dead languages were few and generally not of recent date. Even at the time when the doctrine of Caw-caw was at its height, the death of a language was considered a rare triumph. Since then, many things had changed. The doctrine of the extinction of nations had remained the same, but many of its features were no longer implemented. The Archive now rested content with small victories, which were still held to be important. Even the partial achievement of Nonspeak was a rare success. The process started with the interruption of a language's natural development—reducing it to a kind of mush, like the language spoken by a backward child—and then continued with its further erosion. All the stages of its degradation were noted in a special file: an annual comparison of dictionaries, in which words grew rarer like leaves in November; the ruin of grammar, the withering of particles, especially prefixes, and the coarsening of syntax.

The language began to thicken and stutter. A language like this was almost harmless, because, like a woman with her womb removed, it lost its ability to give birth to stories and legends. The most that it could do from one generation to the next was pass down some dry recollections whose feeble spirit would never stand the test of time.

At that point one of the main stages of Nonspeak was considered complete. Next came what was called the "cold store," or hibernation of the language. This was the onset of chaos and unintelligibility, until the language fell into the deep sleep that preceded its ultimate extinction. As they leafed through the old chronicles that described the final dementia of languages, keen young officials dreamed of bringing back such times of great opportunity. However, a few years of work in the Archive showed them that it took entire generations of human lives for a language to grow old, let alone die. They thanked destiny that the state demanded less and less of them, and more often gave up its insistence on the destruction of the language, resting content if the writers and bards of the subjugated country abandoned their own tongue and wrote in the usual language of the state.

Despite these concessions, work in the linguistic division was the most difficult in the Archive and its staff often applied for transfer to the abolition of national cultures. This was a large section, with innumerable subsections devoted to art, legends, music, mural painting, costumes, wedding customs, choirs, folk epics, and so on. Everything could be

found in its stacks. First there was the loss of color in painting and clothing. The famous scarlet went pale, and blue was
muddied into something Asiatic. Both tended towards ash
gray, the color of serfdom. Then songs became slower and
dances clumsier, until it seemed that the dancers' feet were
shackled. Buildings became less tall, and, of course, writing
was forbidden.

The abolition of national cultures was also the area of
the bitterest controversies. There were still aged veterans
who did not want to change a comma of the centuries-old
laws. Alongside the cursing of a language's alphabet (a rit-
ual whose details had been laid down four centuries before),
they supported, for instance, the cursing of verse forms, nar-
rative prose, fast dancing, and the use of chimneys.

A fresh gust of wind blew, and seemed likely to uproot
the tent. They had every right to complain, Lala Shahini
thought. It was less than a month since the rebel leader had
been beheaded, and the melting snow was still exposing the
occasional corpse. Greece was restless and sharpening its
weapons, and they themselves had come supposedly in order
to destroy the very idea of rebellion, to abolish traditions, to
extirpate the language, and to erase memory. You had to be
slightly dim-witted to believe such twaddle. Just as they had
suspected when they were hastily mustered for their departure, the real reason they had been sent was to cool tempers
in the capital. Indeed, one friend, half joking, had said out-

right before they set off: it seems we're going to banish the idea of rebellion not out there, but here.

The more Lala Shahini thought of it, the crazier their hurried departure on that morning of torrential rain seemed. With their bags crammed to bursting with files and changes of clothes, and their eyes swollen from lack of sleep, they had run like maniacs to the Archive, by whose gate foreign and local journalists were encamped, waiting. The carriages were lined up, and the staff were loading the final chests with documents and maps, while the director himself, the Big Raven, shouted, "Hurry up, hurry up, lads!"

In their confusion, they did not grasp how totally useless this haste had been. They were embarking on a project that would take about two hundred years. But on the road, as their heads nodded and their haunches ached, and especially when they found they had left behind their shaving tackle or sleeping pills, or someone discovered his wife's nightdress mixed up with his underwear, they started accusing first themselves and then the world at large.

During the journey, Lala Shahini had calmed himself by thinking of the larger picture, which was always easy for him. As he drowsed to the creaking of the wheels, events played out in his imagination in different ways, sometimes more dimly, but sometimes in sharp relief. So they were off to quench the spirit of a rebellion. This was no doubt more difficult than extinguishing a volcano. Moreover, rebellions were invisible, he thought, and if they were plugged in one place, they would break out in another, like subterranean gases. Would it not be better to let them erupt, especially in remote territories? Otherwise they could flare up where least expected, increasingly close, until they reached the capital city itself.

He shook himself to get rid of thoughts of this kind. The terrifying Decree of Caw-caw was intended to crush all insurrection above and below the earth. There was even a section, the most secret of all, about subduing the rancor of the dead, which was doubtless the bitterest resentment of all. But apparently only the Big Raven himself dealt with this. Their own duties were confined to horrors aboveground, and they alone were enough to turn your wits.

Like someone trying to tame a kicking horse by exhausting it, Lala Shahini directed his thoughts to the long shelves of files, which seemed to him to spread beyond the edges of the world. They included everything to do with rebellion: the initial signs of discontent, imperceptible to begin with, like the first rats of plague, that appeared softly where you would least imagine, at vegetable stalls, for example, and then the later symptoms, as the rebellion fermented, swelled, and exploded in its intoxicating fury. Then followed its exhaustion and decline, the stupor after large-scale slaughter. Finally came the months, years, and sometimes centuries of searching for and snuffing out every flicker of opposition, until the rebellion's soul was crushed and would never come to life again, and not even its ghost remained.

The enormity of the task made Lala Shahini despair. Sometimes he could see no hope at all on the horizon. As for other depredations such as the dissolution of the language or memory, they were still far away, and never came any closer. These things seemed to dodge out of sight, like crabs. The argument over what should be suppressed first, language or memory, seemed futile. The prospect of wiping out either was so remote. Even more distant was the ultimate goal, the erasure of the nation from the face of the earth, what the chronicles called "reduction to terrain," because this was the ultimate expression of the final purpose: turning a country from a "homeland" to "terrain." Everything had to return to its primal state, to the point where, if one single person retained some faint memory of what had been, he would be considered deluded and taken to a madhouse.

All these matters were enshrined in the secret doctrine. Nobody knew when, where, and still less who had created it. It was said that its source was a secret Mongolian manuscript. Its measures had since been enacted in reality, but some said the manuscript was merely the description of a hallucination, which had emerged from the brain of a monk in the steppes of Bek-Pak-Dala and been unable to go back inside, because the crack in his skull closed. As for the origin of the term *Caw-caw*, this was still more obscure, and it was generally thought to be a remnant of a more explicit expression. It was believed to imitate the cawing of ravens over the featureless terrain: Caw-caw, what nation was here, Caw-caw, where is it now, where did it go? This speculation seemed a little perverse, but in the absence of any other, it was accepted.

Conversation in the big tent lapsed again. The words petered out like in the files of dead languages and the wind seemed to fill the void left by human speech.

One after another, they ordered coffee. Their chief was delayed at the commander-in-chief's lunch. Twice they thought of this lunch, automatically adding "God forbid." The glassy-faced man, his eyes clouded by sleep, still swayed in his seat. Every now and then he seemed about to fall, like a vase, and scatter his scrawny limbs about the tent.

Hurshid Pasha did not lie down to rest as usual after his meal. He had invited to lunch the deputy director of the bank, and, in order not to draw attention to this, had also extended an invitation to two of the fattest and greediest pashas on his staff, as well as to the chief of the delegation from the Archive. Throughout the meal, he forgot, and did not conceal that he had forgotten, the presence of these three others, because his attention was totally focused on the tall banker, whose legs were crossed under the low table like two pitchforks. He was attempting by all means to find out what he could about the reasons behind the search for the so-called remainder of the treasure. But it had been impossible. Not only had he failed to discover anything, but the matter seemed even more obscure. The banker had been inscrutable. From under his eyebrows, Hurshid Pasha studied the man's head, so curiously small for that lanky body. It was topped by a huge turban, in whose folds nestled an oval piece of glass, an imitation ruby like some motionless eye. This monstrous eye had agitated Hurshid Pasha throughout the meal, as if it were to blame for his failure to connect with the man under the turban. In fact, Hurshid Pasha had never seen a man whose features were so thoroughly effaced by his headgear. The turban had usurped his guest's real face, and the mouth, nose, and especially his eyes were mere accessories. To come to terms with this man meant first dealing with the turban, and in particular with that unblinking eye planted like some gland among its folds.

Hurshid Pasha had never endured such a disagreeable lunch. At times he had felt an overwhelming desire to tear off that filthy turban, throw it to the ground, and say to this man with the tiny eyes: Now that you're without your turban, tell me why you're really looking for the rest of the treasure. Have you really worked out the figures, and do you think there is more of it, or do you know yourself that there's nothing and this is only a pretext?

When the lunch was over at last, Hurshid Pasha went outside for a walk. It would soon be evening. The field was covered with frost and the plains beyond were still dusted with floury snow. Out in the open, his gloomy thoughts evaporated, and his anxiety might have vanished completely if it were not for one small matter that drummed in his mind, as though tapping against a piece of wood in his head. This is not possible, he told himself. The sovereign could not do that. "My son," he had written in his last letter, "I know that you will not sleep until you send me the rebel's head. My devoted subject, this is the only gift that I will ever expect from you." It isn't possible, Hurshid Pasha thought again, listening to the frost crunch under his feet. I defeated the rebel and delivered his head. The whole world was talking about Hurshid Pasha. It was totally impossible. These were only insane suspicions, which a crazy lunch like this merely magnified.

Dusk was falling. The broad plain had now absorbed all the world's misery. That round lunch table, that circle of delirium to which his flailing mind had been pinned a short time ago, seemed far away.

What a good thing that he had gone out for a walk. The frost crackled, *krak kruk*, under his heels. It was the earth that had won. This sound more than anything else conveyed a sense of triumph.

He was the man of the moment, and the newspapers were writing about him continually. His friend the minister Gizer had sent him some cuttings with the latest post. The empire's strongman, who had restored the glory of Ottoman arms. The general of the day. But as his eyes skimmed those long headlines full of compliments, he had wondered with a dim, obscure distress if the typeface wasn't a bit too large.

He had thrust aside this doubt at once. Ahead of him lay the state dinners in honor of the victory, and celebrations, new promotions. The grand vizier was said to suffer from an ulcer, and his position . . . Perhaps those above him really thought that Ali's treasure had been larger. What could you expect from people who calculated such things, like this sinister deputy director, whom he shouldn't have invited to lunch at all?

It was cold. The twilight was thickening. Ali's widow must have arrived in the capital by now. One could imagine the general curiosity, the speculation of the journalists, the ladies' envy.

He felt homesick for the capital. Like a warm wind, his memory brought back to him a fragment of its night sky, with the pale eternal smoldering lights of its minarets and the towers of its palaces, in which the city's beautiful ladies slept. I'm tired, he said to himself. I need some entertainment.

He felt astonishingly relieved.

That's why people relax in fresh air, he thought after a little. Their anxieties fly away, evaporate . . . but perhaps they don't disappear. A worry can be felt in the atmosphere. It seems that space absorbs people's excessive gloom, keeps it to itself for a while, and suspends it like mist above us all until it finds a chance to redistribute it.

If they really didn't believe there was more treasure, why were they doing this? Why? He did all he could to banish this bitter thought, but in the end he let it settle on his mind. Was the Padishah perhaps scared of people who received too much praise? The newspaper headlines quickly fell into ranks in his mind. Then for a moment it seemed to him that he was running among their black letters as if they were mousetraps. Take for yourself the excessive praise, my liege, he imagined himself saying. Take it all, if you want, what is excessive and what isn't. Just don't destroy me.

He astonished himself with this cry from his soul. What did it mean? He was alone in the black, dusk-shrouded plain. Was his sovereign replacing his generals with stupid but loyal pashas? Or maybe . . .

Enough, he thought. How chickenhearted. For the moment, you are lord of this entire conquered province.

The frost crunched under his feet as before.

For a while he walked on, empty, a nameless, spiritless moving form, over this wasteland carrying the burden of that winter.

That must be it, he said to himself.

Krak kruk, went the frost underneath him, and he was on the point of asking out loud what that "it" could be.

The deputy director of the bank had departed for the capital, and all sorts of couriers had left and come back bearing messages with seals of every rank. Other officials with long and elaborate titles had arrived, as well as delegates from the Palace of the Registrar looking into Ali's properties, undercover envoys from the centuries-old Palace of Psst-Psst, staff from the First Directorate of the Sheikh-ul-Islam, messengers from the Palace of Dreams in their blue-painted carriages or *tabir arabalar*, "vehicles of interpretation," and dervishes traveling for reasons unknown to anyone. These people brought huge dossiers of documents, orders, and instructions, but nothing about the treasure of the defeated vizier.

Hurshid Pasha was perpetually drowsy. Around him,

the world seemed to pulse like some viscous gray mass with trembling pink veins within it. Life went on, orders were given and sent back, but Hurshid Pasha was half asleep.

One day, while taking his usual walk at dusk, his feet paused involuntarily by a hut at whose entrance was written the word *tabir*, "interpretation." According to the regulations, these offices were set up in all the major army encampments, with the duty, among other tasks, to collect and interpret dreams. Those dreams that were connected to the outcomes of military operations were sent immediately to headquarters. Other dreams of more general import were sent off to the capital, to the famous Palace of Dreams, or Tabir Saray.

Hurshid Pasha had paid no attention to these offices, just as he had been indifferent to the offices of the pronouncers of curses, the astrologers, the sorcerers, the gunsmiths, and more recently the exorcists of spyglasses, who, like every new profession, were highly valued. Preoccupied by dozens of other matters, he had forgotten the interpreters of dreams entirely, until now, looking at the word *tabir* written in sky blue by the entrance to the hut, it seemed to him that he had stumbled across a quaint relic.

He pushed open the door and entered. The two clerks inside bowed to the ground. They knew that he had paid no attention to their interpretations of dreams, even when the fortune of the war had hung by a thread, and he would hardly worry about them now that it was all over. Previously, these men's lives had been ruled by fear. There had been little dreaming, and of those dreams sent to them, many had been valueless. The clerks were scared that if the war were lost, a storm of recrimination might fall on them. Two days before Ali's death, they had seen with horror that their morning file was empty. In the hope of producing something, an entire battalion was then ordered to sleep under the threat of the whip. But the results cast the interpreters into deeper despair: most of the soldiers saw no dreams, and the others recounted mere nonsense.

The clerks remained bowed in front of the pasha.

"At your service, my lord," stammered one of them at last.

Hurshid Pasha stretched out his hand to the shelf where the files were.

"Have you got a dream for me?" he asked, trying to make his voice as casual or even as sarcastic as possible.

The clerks leaped to the files and opened them eagerly. They talked continually as they riffled through the pages, interrupting each other, reading a line here and there, and muttering under their breath: "A minaret, with a few flies buzzing around it . . . no, no, wait, the dream of Janissary Selim from the Third Battalion, look, here it is, we still haven't sent it to headquarters, but it has no connection to you, my lord. Tomorrow, we'll send it with the first courier."

Hurshid Pasha paid no attention to their muttering but watched their shaking hands as they leafed through the files. He imagined the pale blue towers of the Tabir Saray, towards which dream couriers were hurrying in their similarly pale blue carriages from all the corners of the empire. He tried to remember everything he could about this monstrous institution, but his recollections were vague. All sorts of things were said about the mysterious scrutiny of dreams in its innumerable offices and how omens were extracted from them. Now he was sorry that he had not been more attentive.

Hurshid Pasha, his hands crossed on his chest, watched as they wildly combed the files.

Strange, he said to himself, without knowing why, and he left the hut so quietly that the clerks failed to notice. Had some dream about him been delivered from some remote corner of the state, he wondered. Why else was he shaking like this, to the core of his being?

He tried to put the idea out of his head, and walked on for a while, but his thoughts kept returning to where he least wanted them. Whatever it was that coursed through his mind, it was something impalpable and distant. Dusk was falling. He tried to imagine how at this moment, at nightfall, the whole imperial land mass, for whose expansion he had fought all his life, was crisscrossed by dream couriers, like blue comets.

Hurshid Pasha felt sleepy.

This somnolent state, which Hurshid Pasha would have liked to prolong for the rest of his life, was unexpectedly interrupted on Friday. He received a letter delivered by private messenger from his friend the minister Gizer, who had casually added at the very end: "It gives me no pleasure to tell you that the day after tomorrow a courier of the court's Third Branch is setting off with a decree for you that bodes no good. Judge and decide for yourself. As the wise Ibn Sina said, the world is everywhere under the stars. I salute you and I would rather we never met again than for me to see you and you not see me."

Hurshid Pasha held this letter in front of his eyes for a long time. As if he were outside his own body, he detected a muffled, almost silent wrangling, a perpetual *psst-psst* taking place among his various parts, which were no longer coordinated but at odds with one another. His lungs sent nothing to his mouth, his hands tried in vain to link up directly with his brain, and his palate, fingers, spine—they were all totally numb. At last, with an effort, he managed to impose a sort of approximate order. This was what he had expected.

He made a simple calculation. The letter had been written three days ago. Gizer had been careful to ensure that it reached him as soon as possible. In the meantime, Tundj Hata would have departed. Two days' grace, he thought. His mind grasped hold of this concept as if it were a handle. A two-day period. A length of time consisting of two days. So, two days' grace. And then what? he wondered dully. What sort of time came after that?

Again after a great effort, the creaking, bickering components of his being began to communicate with one another. Two days to save his skin, he thought. Gizer had told him plainly, "I would rather we never met again than for me to see you and you not see me." This was an almost transparent allusion to the Traitor's Niche.

Two days' grace, he repeated to himself, as if measuring its sufficiency for a specific task. His instinct of survival cried softly inside him, ah, if only there were more time. But then it struck him that there was enough time, indeed too much. It began to look terrifyingly protracted. Better not to have this two days' grace at all. This was a hostile two-headed monster. What use was it, except to torture him? Gizer was subtly advising him to flee abroad, but he ruled out this idea at once. To live in Europe, under the sign of the cross—this was like swapping a wolf for a snake. Better here among the dead under the age-old royal earth, where the crescent moon dripped its yellow light to the ground like balm, rather than alive and over there.

He burned his friend's letter and went outside. It was the same plain, the same frost breaking *krak-kruk* under his heels. The clouds had climbed higher in the sky, leaving room for a little more daylight to pass through them. He thought of Ali Pasha. How many will you drag down after you? He looked at the far horizon, where there had been mist since the start of the war. From which direction would Tundj Hata appear? he wondered.

Hurshid Pasha focused his eyes on the broad expanse of the sky, as if the courier in his carriage with the royal arms could sweep down through the clouds like Gabriel. But then his eyes wandered to the road. It was barely imaginable that such horror could come to him down this frail, narrow track.

He could not rid his mind of a tumult of horses, filthy Tatars, salt buckets, snow, honey, and silver dishes. He imagined his own head under the arm of Tundj Hata, and strangely this thought did not terrify him but drew tears. Amid his weeping, he recalled the silvery gleam of a fish head.

He pressed the palms of his hands to wipe his cheeks. You will be taken far away, he muttered to his own head. You will travel alone. Again he imagined his head pressed against the courier's leather jerkin. The head of a six-times-decorated pasha under the arm of a middle-ranking civil servant.

No. It won't happen. Besides, on the day of the Last Judgment, when the trumpet of Allah sounds and all rise from the grave, where would he find his head, removed thousands of miles away? What would he do without it? He imagined himself standing paralyzed and headless at a crossroads, pushed by the crowds of the dead, each running to their own place, and again he said to himself, no, Tundj Hata, you won't get me.

Now it all seemed simple to him. With brisk steps he went back to the tent, took ink and paper out of the chest, and started writing his last wishes. The first and most important was that he must be buried at once on the morning of the next day, before dawn, and without a funeral ceremony. Next, his grave must be five fathoms deep and not an inch less. His third instruction was about the division of his wealth. He spent a long time not on the portions to be left to his family, which were easily settled, but on bequests for the salvation of his soul. For some reason he remembered a mausoleum he had seen in his youth on the Albanian coast near the old naval base of Pashaliman, among some desolate sand dunes. Since then he had seen many magnificent graves and tombs all over the empire, but nothing had erased the impression of that forlorn mausoleum and its lamp, burning day and night for the salvation of the soul of a certain Mirahor Pasha, a former commander of the base. So he left instructions in his will for such a mausoleum to be built for the benefit of his soul. He started writing down the sums of money required for its construction, the daily wage of the keeper, the lamp oil . . . but ground to a halt in this last calculation of his life. What proportion of his wealth should be set aside for the maintenance of his tomb and for lamp oil for two hundred and eighty, three hundred and twenty, four hundred and ninety, six hundred and sixty years? The time he would spend dead was long, subject to different and totally confusing measurements. He tried to make some kind of approximate forecast, and several times wrote and erased the figures at the end of his will, but still he did not feel sure. Indeed, when he sealed the letter and prostrated himself on the little prayer rug, he was haunted by that little wick in the desolate mausoleum in the first chill of autumn. Two or three times he made as if to stand up to make a correction, but he was too tired.

Towards dusk, the guards on duty outside the tent heard the gunshot and rushed inside.

•

The courier arrived on Sunday afternoon, three days after leaving the capital. As if urged on by a premonition of disaster, Tundj Hata had covered the distance at incredible speed. Even so, when he arrived, Hurshid Pasha had already been buried for nearly forty hours.

The carriage had not yet stopped when from behind the horses' straining muscles, flexing joints, foaming mouths, and flaring manes the newly hennaed beard of Tundj Hata could be seen, wavering like a flame.

"Where is he?" he wailed.

Even from outside, he could sense the tent was empty.

"Hey, guard! Is there a guard here?"

One of the pasha's guards came out.

"Where is your master?" cried Tundj Hata.

The guard's eyes were calm. He pointed to the sky.

"He is there, sir, have you still not heard?"

I suspected as much, Tundj Hata groaned to himself. You miserable creature. So this is what you wanted to do to me after your death. For a few moments, Tundj Hata went berserk with his whip, striking the guard and the horses, which barely remained on their feet, and then his Tatars, raising a cloud of dust from their backs.

He calmed down a little and took out the *Regulations* from his saddlebag, leafing through it many times before he found what he wanted. It was Chapter Four: "Cases in Which the Person Condemned by Decree Lays Hands upon Himself,

Before the Sentence of Death Is Delivered." He read this ten times until he thought he understood it.

"Take me to his grave," he cried.

They led him to it. He walked crazily in a circle around the grave, as if looking for a secret entrance, and gave the order to open it.

Hehehe, he chuckled to himself, as the sextons threw the soil to each side. You thought you had got away from me, hehehe.

The exhumation took a long time. There was no sign of the body. "It's been stolen," he kept crying out, "you wretches." They explained to him that they had buried him deep, because that's what he had wanted. They had been surprised. What was this strange request? Five fathoms deep, but now, ah now, it was obvious why . . . "There'll be trouble for you if you don't find him," he persisted, paying them no attention. "A curse on the mothers who bore you!"

At a depth of precisely five fathoms, the diggers struck the wood of the coffin. It was still day when they pulled the body out with the help of a rope, which was tied to an iron ring with three hooks. One of the hooks had run through the dead man's back, piercing his cloak. They dumped the muddy body, almost folded in two, on the pile of earth beside the grave. Tundj Hata decapitated the corpse with two blows of his yataghan, taking no care not to soil himself or the head.

He set off for the capital city that same night.

7

Neither Frontier nor Center, Caw-Caw.
Then the Center and the End

THE ROYAL courier's carriage devoured the miles at a crazy speed. Now and again, Tundj Hata poked his head out the small window to remind the Tatars how late they were. He wanted to make up, at any cost, at least half of those lost forty hours that the head of Hurshid Pasha had spent under the earth attached to his corpse and without medical supervision.

As he studied the continental plain that stretched desolately in front of him, Tundj Hata tried to work out how much time he would gain by not showing the severed head. This was not easy, because quite apart from his exhaustion, he couldn't determine where he was. The road they had been following for many hours, like all the roads that passed through terrain with no identity, had milestones without numbers.

They were still in Provinces Two, Six, and Seven. Organized on the principle of Caw-caw, the territories had no other names and these numbers denoted them in official documents and in the press. The royal road passed fastidiously through these regions as if in disgust, passing stupefied villages and towns on whose streets wandered people clad in gray, stammering in their clumsy tongue as if they had suffered strokes.

These people no longer had their own languages, customs, colors, weddings, scripts, or calendars. Their memory had been slowly worn away and everything had been expunged from it. Their lives came to resemble those plains, whipped by the wind for a thousand centuries on end and finally reduced to a forlorn nothingness where there were only sand dunes, whose interminable undulations stretched monotonously into the distance, always the far distance.

Indeed these people's entire lives were strangely bound in a noose that led them nowhere yet never let them go. Long ago they had lost all sense of time and space, concepts that had become like some shapeless and useless pulp.

Everything about these people was soft and mushy, from their clothes—for not only were colors forbidden but also the use of buttons, collars, belts, and anything that tightened a garment (according to Caw-caw the clothing in this terrain had to resemble the shape of a stripped animal skin)—to their speech. After the death of their language, they used a kind of debased version of the usual language of the state. It was an impoverished patois of only two or three hundred words. Because of the blurring of particles and prefixes, the words were not linked to one another but merely arranged like beads on a string that could be put together in any order.

To say "I'm going to the fold to milk the sheep," they might say "go fold milk sheep" or "fold sheep milk go" and so on. In this way the language crumbled like pumice or loose gravel, always changing its shape.

When a terrain entered its deep slumber, its institutions, police, courts, postal services, and record offices were abolished and only a few semireligious, semifinancial civil servants were left, dealing mainly with tax collection. Like their subjects, with the passage of time these officials forgot dates and years until even the harvesting of taxes and all the other tasks of government were performed like bodily functions. From one year to the next, weights and measures were forgotten, so that people said "a cartload of corn" for a quantity of grain or "as far as a mare can gallop" for a distance. "A bellyful of bread" expressed the quantity of food that could fill a person, and so forth.

The police and other institutions were abolished so that this slumber would not be disturbed by any memory of power. Indeed, the capital considered it necessary to brainwash its officials, because only if they shared the collective trance could it be ensured that they would not rouse the population from their sleep with some sudden motion or thought.

Tundj Hata had been passing through Provinces Two, Six, and Seven for the last four years without anybody finding out about his performances. Sometimes, as he looked out through the carriage windows at that sequence of villages and settlements, some close and others distant, he felt attracted by their deathly calm. People said that there were many high officials, weary of political scheming and infighting, who felt the lure of these degraded territories. In some cases they left everything behind and departed for them, and were mourned in their lifetimes by friends and relatives. They never came back, or in the rare cases when a few did return, they were less than ghosts of their former selves and so entirely altered (not even bodies left under the earth in the solitude of death underwent such a transformation) that they were merely objects of pity. Even this pity was of a different kind, a sly, treacherous sort of sympathy. These returnees were neither of sound mind nor mad, neither entirely present nor absent. They were more than corrupted: they had made a kind of down payment on death, and had a kind of intimacy with death that nobody else possessed. They were like carriers of some mysterious disease that might infect everything—people and buildings—causing sores and troubled sleep.

As he traveled, Tundj Hata never took his eyes from the carriage window. He was one of those few people who entered and left these desolate regions on business. He was familiar with this death manifested in the arable fields, haystacks, and chimneyless dwellings. He had never understood why the first step should be the destruction of chimneys, but the ancient chronicles related that when a village or town woke to find its chimneys destroyed, the inhabitants would shriek in horror: "Caw-caw."

Whenever he passed through this somnolent region of the state, Tundj Hata involuntarily recalled other regions that were the total opposite: the provinces in a "state of emergency." Whenever his duties took him through these parts, not only did it not occur to him to show his severed heads but, although he was escorted by a guard, he did not dare stop anywhere or even stretch his head out of the carriage.

These were dangerous regions, which, for different reasons, could not be handed over to the army to be subdued by brute force, nor subjected to Caw-caw. Because neither of these solutions was possible, these provinces were placed under the responsibility of the First Directorate of the Interior Ministry.

In the coffee-colored ministry building, innumerable civil servants worked day and night on the problem of these areas. Here they brewed major conflicts within nations, centuries-old enmities, feuds, and hatred. Here they stoked religious discord, linguistic quarrels, provocations by plainsmen against mountain dwellers, mainlanders against islanders, northerners against southerners, and everyone against everyone else.

In these regions, there was no end to the turmoil and terror. Everything was in a perpetually flushed and excited state, from the colors of people's clothing, which never matched, to the language, which was always spoken differently in every province according to whim, sometimes nasally, sometimes gutturally, or with word order reversed. The populations fought all the time about everything, quarreling over pastures, the shape of roofs, the style of cloaks, the names of the seasons, and especially customs. Some people, to spite their neighbors, turned marriage rites into funeral rites, and others, out of malice, did the opposite.

The orgy of fury knew no limits, especially on festival days. Travelers passing through these parts would be terrified out of their skins. It was not for nothing that old people referred to these regions as "smoldering fires." That new word *hotbed*, which the bright sparks of the capital city uttered so proudly, as they did all words borrowed from Europe, was only a translation of this.

It was believed that after twenty or twenty-five years of this treatment, these provinces would be totally exhausted and would beg for the respite of sleep. Then the Directorate would hand them over to the Central Archive, to be put under the rule of Caw-caw.

Tundj Hata was one of the few people in a position to compare these smoldering regions with the Caw-caw territories. Last time he had passed through, the people had bitten his carriage with their teeth, and then, failing to overturn it, had thrown acid at it from a distance.

Never again by that route, he muttered to himself whenever his carriage covered the final miles. A hundred times better by this road, he thought again as his head nodded in sleep. They make me welcome here. Perhaps I am the only person they ever welcome.

Indeed, the villages and settlements, stretching miserably in their winter lethargy, had been waiting weeks and months for his henna-stained beard to appear, red against the snow. And as they waited, the image of a severed human head was like a kernel, like some long-unfertilized cell planted inside them.

On some kind of afternoon in some sort of month but in no season, and of course in no year (it was remembered that it was cold, no more), a man from far away, a strange courier with the royal emblems on his chest, had stopped just to show them something, for free. And because they had eyes to see, they turned them towards this thing, which was a human head. Then the courier had gone, without a word to them and without listening to anything they said. After a while, for reasons they did not understand, they felt troubled in their minds. It was a feeling of expectation, something they had never experienced in their lives, and for which there was not even a word in their language.

This head had set in motion something inside them. Something stirred weakly, faintly, deep in the dark corners of their memory, but without surfacing.

On the second occasion, the courier showed them the head for only a very short time, but gave them an explanation for it. This was the head of a pasha, he told them, but they understood nothing of what he said. It took a long time to convince them that a pasha might be without a head.

The third time, when he noticed their eyes fixed impatiently on his leather saddlebags, he asked them for money.

From then on, the severed heads became events of a kind, which drew together the threads of their lives. They became markers, dividing lines, and in the end a kind of calendar. The habit began of remembering incidents in relation to them:

this or that happened around the time of that elderly head, or a little after that frost-covered head. Later, head sightings were remembered like heavenly signs, like eclipses, comets, or meteorological disasters. There were heads that separated two seasons (for these people thought they needed something to mark the division of the seasons), there was the head of the second snowfall, and, finally, the head of the gales.

There were women who fell in love with them, as happened with the head of the "blond pasha." They mainly asked, "Where was this head cut?" The question of why came only later, much later. There was no way they could understand what rebellion meant, still less a general insurrection, but Tundj Hata was careful to give them some sort of story, to make his show more attractive. He found it difficult to come up with a simple way to explain the state hierarchy to them, so that he could take payment for the heads according to their importance. They grasped the idea finally, and even started demanding heads of higher rank. But he knew how to play to them: he would vanish for whole weeks or threaten to suspend the shows, wildly spurring on his horses on the black highway, leaving the villagers behind with their lanterns casting yellow patches of light on the snow.

For days and weeks, people who had not known what it meant to wait found themselves trapped in suspense. Like a hook lowered into the depths of a well, the severed head dangled near those things that had perished in the distant past: stale ballads, neglected heroic songs, long-forgotten wars. The head disturbed these things at the bottom of this well, but could not catch hold of them and draw them to the surface. The people, when they stood frozen and wide-eyed in front of the head, felt this muffled and mysterious struggle deep within themselves as a form of anguish, like some rare mineral buried in the depths of the earth, a groan of misery tinged with a bitterness that surfaced in their daily lives only in dreams.

After Tundj Hata's departure, they fell into a stupor for days on end. A terrifying blankness settled over entire villages, as if they had been struck by epilepsy. The head was far away in Tundj Hata's carriage, but the memory of it remained with them for a long time. It was planted in their thoughts, like some sort of cabbage thrown into the black earth. There were countries where heads rose up and were then cut down. There were disturbed countries. There was a country called Shqipëria, a name that could be translated more or less as a convocation of eagles with bloodstained plumage scattered by the winds and storms.

One morning, a peasant of Province Six was found face-down on the rush matting of his own hut, his clothes shredded, his hair torn out, and wounds on his face from his own fingernails. He was still alive, but unable to give any explanation of why he had done this. After a while, he tried to express himself, but his story, confused in itself, reached listeners' ears in an even more garbled form. The gist was that he had wrestled with himself all night. It had been a dreadful struggle, as if his enemy had been his own lungs, nerves, and veins. The man tried to explain how he had grappled with the words of the language. They had been heavy and so stubborn, and he had wanted to dislodge them from their old masonry to realign them in a new order, but this had been difficult, so difficult, he groaned, showing his bloody and broken nails. "Oh, it was impossible, they almost strangled me," he said, showing the marks on his throat.

People listened and shrugged their shoulders and went away with bowed heads. Others came and looked at this man who was dying and couldn't tell who had killed him. There was no way they could understand that this person, for the first time since the last of their ballads had disappeared almost two hundred years ago, had been trying to compose a new one.

Tundj Hata entered the capital city by the Seventh Gate just before midnight. The guards opened the doors, muttering curses and yawning, and pulled themselves together only when they saw his papers under the light of the lantern.

"Another head," one of them said, when the carriage had clattered away deep into the city. "What's going on?"

"Why so surprised? Don't you read the newspapers?" the other man replied.

Meanwhile the carriage wheels made a deafening sound through the sleeping streets. In the darkness, the high walls of the government buildings loomed over the road. Lanterns dimly illuminated iron gates with handles in the form of human hands. On that cold March night, it seemed as if the emptiness of the silent, deserted passages behind the gates would seep out through their keyholes like black liquid.

The carriage rattled across the Square of the Ottoman Crescent, past the gates of the Imperial Bank and the grim building of the Foreign Ministry. In the distance, under the rising moon, the Obelisk of Tokmakhan appeared, painfully illuminated by a faint gleam that suggested the ethereal voice of some creature, whose plaintive tears misted it from tip to toe.

The inner trembling that Tundj Hata experienced whenever he returned from a mission and entered the capital made his teeth chatter. The closed gates with black keyholes, through which it seemed all life had drained away, made him shiver. What had happened during his absence? he wondered. It must be something terrible. They might tell him, for instance, that he was late, or they might have heard about his head displays. Or, worse, some disaster might have befallen them simply because he wasn't there.

The carriage passed the gloomy lead-roofed palace of the Sheikh-ul-Islam. Its walls seemed to reflect back the noise of the wheels, angrily casting it back against Tundj Hata. Glued to the window and with a tightened heart, he looked at the great government buildings as they passed by in the semidarkness. There was the menacing bronze gable of the War Ministry. There were the gates of the Fourth Directorate. The long walls of the prison of the "Accursed Courtyard" were not far from the towers of the Palace of Dreams. For a while the carriage wheels rumbled alongside the rectangular palace of the Great Registry, in whose ancient ledgers, it was said, all the empire's real estate, every property large or small, was listed. Tundj Hata sighed, without knowing why. It was said that in this registry everything had a number, whether it was an inn, a mausoleum, an olive tree, or an entire ocean. Everything—field, sea, or olive tree—had a number. Tundj Hata sighed even more deeply. He felt like this whenever he was confronted by the majesty of the state, and his sense of its greatness was never stronger than when he returned from a mission at night.

Here was the Temple of the Ottoman Spirit, and there was the western corner of the Admiralty, with the six-story building of the First Directorate immediately behind it. They were all in their places, as they always had been and always would be, heavy grindstones ceaselessly turning.

Yet out there—the thought made him laugh—far away, a few Albanians wanted to bring down this might.

Tundj Hata would have released a guffaw if he hadn't been in the capital city, whose walls seemed to press on his temples. Out there far away . . . he repeated to himself two or three times. There were Hungarians, Albanians, Serbs, Greeks, Croats, Romanians, and a swarm of other non-Islamic peoples. Out there . . . a vague, obscure anxiety lapped at his consciousness.

He had slowly become familiar with this anxiety during his long missions, racing by day and by night through the interminable expanses of this centuries-old state. Its provinces, governments, and great pashadoms stretched away one after another. The innumerable peoples of the empire lay spread out, each in their own lands and with their own fate. As faint as a distant galaxy in autumn, inscrutable, remote, their regions covered with indifference like frost, the thought of them made him huddle inside his carriage as he flew through their provinces like the north wind. There were times when, amid this multitude of peoples, the palaces and columns and towers of the capital looked small to him, like children's toys. These were brief moments and he laughed at himself afterwards for his weakness, as if he had been scared by a dream. But recently the bitter taste of this anxiety, which usually vanished as soon as he drew near the capital, had lingered.

It was this that really prevented Tundj Hata from laughing out loud into the night.

He wiped the steam of his breath from the carriage window and tried to work out which street they had taken, but could not. The carriage stopped at last in front of the house of the chief medical officer, Evrenos, who was also the court's protocol officer. The procedure was to wake this doctor immediately when heads arrived late at night, to avoid the slightest delay in supplying medical attention.

One of the Tatars knocked loudly at the gate. It was a heavy gate of oak, braced with iron. As at all houses where senior officials lived, there was a lantern fixed to the wall beside it.

Tundj Hata stepped from his carriage and paced up and down the street to stretch his legs. The house was in darkness; the Tatar knocked again. Tundj Hata saw a torn newspaper, thrown on the street. He bent down, picked it up, and tried to read it under the low light of the lantern. The decree condemning Hurshid Pasha had been published. Tundj Hata screwed up his eyes and made out a few words here and there. Something about the sequestration of Ali's treasure.

The Tatar knocked for the third time. Tundj Hata could also discern the name of Ali Pasha's widow in the society column. Below this, the price of bronze had fallen again.

Finally, a voice replied from inside the house:

"Who is it?"

"A servant of the state, looking for Chief Medical Officer Evrenos," Tundj Hata called out.

"He's not here," the voice replied.

"Don't lie to me," said Tundj Hata. "Wake him up at once. It's important."

The voice speaking through the grille insisted that the master of the house was not there. Tundj Hata finally accepted that he had been invited to an after-dinner party. He noted the name of the street and the house number and set off at once.

It was an hour past midnight. The carriage wheels rumbled even more loudly on the paving. Tundj Hata touched the leather bag. Did you ever think that this is how you would return to the capital? he silently asked the severed head. You imagined entering in triumph on a white horse, with music and speeches, but here you are in a saddlebag. Here I am carrying you from door to door before I hand you over.

The house where the chief medical officer was dining

appeared dark, but a ray of light came from the garden. The Tatars took turns knocking until someone opened the gate. The man who answered was tipsy and barely understood what they wanted. Eventually he grasped the gist and went to look for the doctor. Yet on his way up the stairs he must have forgotten his errand, because nobody came back out. Tundj Hata pushed the gate that the drunk man had left half open and entered.

He climbed the stairs and followed two or three cold corridors and saw the whole company through a glass door, in a room strewn with rugs, in front of a hearth with a glowing fire.

"My dear Tundj Hata," Chief Medical Officer Evrenos called out. "Come in and let me introduce you to my friends."

Tundj Hata shook his head. He whispered something in Evrenos's ear, while the other diners looked in horror at this phantom, white with dust, that had suddenly appeared among them.

"Take a glass of raki, sir," one of them said in a trembling voice, perhaps wanting to test if this uninvited guest were really human.

Tundj Hata did not even turn his head. Dr. Evrenos finally understood the purpose of the visit, sobered up instantly, and asked for his cloak.

They busied themselves getting ready. Shutting the glass door, they left behind the glowing fire, the excited faces of the guests, a little dampened here and there, and whispers: Who is it? Someone so sick that they call Evrenos at this time? Some vizier for sure. Yes, yes, it must be a member of the government.

"We must wake the Keeper of Poisons," Evrenos said, climbing into the carriage. "He will issue the embalming fluids."

Tundj Hata did not answer. Let them follow all the rules, he thought. His duty was to bring the head all the way from the frontier of the state. There were other people to deal with the rest. After the Keeper of Poisons, they would wake the Chief of Protocol, who also had to be present when the head was delivered.

Get them all, then, Tundj Hata thought, annoyed and a little hurt. It's easy to make a face at the sight of this head, but try fetching one yourself. Ride hundreds of miles through the cold winter, only to find the man you're looking for already dead and buried. Five fathoms deep. He had handled this alone.

Trrak, trrak trrak . . . one of the Tatars knocked at the gate of the Keeper of Poisons.

Let the Keeper of Poisons come, or the keeper of boiled sweets, but don't argue with Tundj Hata, he muttered to himself. He was in the state of rage that he always suffered before handing over a head, especially when he suspected that there would be problems with the delivery, as there usually were. The protocol staff would argue about the appearance of the head, possible scratches and especially the firmness of the flesh. Everyone wanted to keep to the rules of his own job, and paid no attention to anyone else's.

The Keeper of Poisons, holding his enormous bag, climbed into the carriage as if drunk.

"To the Chief of Protocol," said Tundj Hata and the doctor almost in one voice, as they bunched closer together to make room for the new passenger.

Now we'll shake this little bird out of his nest too, Tundj Hata said to himself.

The carriage wheels rattled like chains through the midnight streets. The head of the Keeper of Poisons, no doubt fast asleep again, nodded back and forth. Tundj Hata wanted to shout: Wake up, servants of the state, leave your warm feather beds. Look at this cabbage I've brought you! But he knew he could not hand it over yet, and his excitement subsided.

Trrak, trrak, trrak, the Tatars knocked at the tall and narrow gate of the Chief of Protocol.

Tundj Hata touched his bag. My pasha, did you ever imagine coming to the capital like this? Hurshid Pasha, carried from door to door, knocking here, knocking there. Let's see if they'll take you in.

He felt something resembling a perverted kind of sympathy.

The Chief of Protocol finally came out, thin, gray-haired, sleepy, his locks poking out from under a carelessly donned turban.

He climbed into the carriage, which set off for the Directorate of Protocol, where he would now deliver the head. The clock in a nearby square chimed two.

Again the carriage drove along a street lined with government buildings. The Palace of Seals and Decrees. The Islamic Academy. Tundj Hata trembled. To his right he made out the wing of a somber building that appeared powdered with leaden dust: the centuries-old Palace of Psst-Psst.

Tundj Hata instinctively tensed whenever he passed in front of it. The thought that someone might have made a report about him from the regions where he gave his displays made his flesh creep. At times he thought that some hint must have arrived but, fortunately, remained filed among billions of other rumors whispered from one person to another, the stale gossip and tittle-tattle that millions of mouths passed on.

Without turning his head, Tundj Hata sensed the wall of this repulsive palace still looming to the right of the carriage. Oh God, he said to himself, everything is there. His hand touched the saddlebag. No doubt your rumors, too, my pasha.

Tundj Hata shivered again, imagining the reverberation of rumors coming from the depths of the earth, from graves and tombs topped with stone turbans. The files of the age-old Palace of Psst-Psst were said to contain everything that anybody, anywhere, had whispered at any time during the last eight hundred years.

Tundj Hata breathed again in relief. They had left the palace behind with the roar of its thousands of files, like the waves on an infinite sandy beach. The empire makes a noise, the director of the palace, Izgurlu Effendi, was reputed to say whenever the long-standing sickness of his right ear was mentioned.

Let him go deaf, Tundj Hata silently cursed him, and touched the saddlebag again. My pasha, perhaps this palace was your downfall too.

The carriage, its lanterns now extinguished, drove down some narrow lanes and stopped in front of the Directorate of Protocol. They all entered the building. Clasping the saddlebag, Tundj Hata forgot about the Palace of Psst-Psst. The blind fury that had gripped him a short time earlier took hold of him again. The delivery took a long time. The officials argued about the condition of the head, and although Tundj Hata waved the exhumation certificate at them, proving that the body had been under the earth for forty hours, they would not believe it, but carefully examined the cheeks, bringing a lamp close to the eyes of the deceased pasha, and sighing.

Finally, the two parties reached a sort of agreement: the head was accepted, but the delivery note was heavily annotated with the head's flaws, and the exhumation certificate was attached.

When everything was done, Tundj Hata and the Chief of Protocol left, while Evrenos and the Keeper of Poisons remained behind to treat the head.

So that is all, Tundj Hata thought as he pushed open the door of his house. There had been no shouting or celebrations to welcome him back to the city, only a few knocks on doors at midnight before his saddlebag was passed from one hand to another.

His small house was surrounded by a garden. The moon shone on the bare branches of the almond trees, silvered with frost. It was a clear, crisp light that came from high above, beyond the reach of human hands and minds.

Tundj Hata stood still, staring at this icy lacework. He was totally exhausted, but thought he could stay for a few moments like this. On his right hip, he felt at the same time an absence and the touch of something, such as a patient feels after the removal of a tumor. He understood and took a deep breath. He was relieved after delivering the head. Now Evrenos and the Keeper of Poisons are decking you out for your wedding day, he thought. The frost-covered branches of the almond tree scattered indifferent sparks of light like jewels.

He felt that this bath of moonlight was rinsing the pollution of death from his body. He took out his key and slowly opened the gate. Inside it was dark and warm.

He heard the gently tremulous voice of his wife: "Tundj, is that you?"

"Yes," he replied, almost in a sigh.

After a moment, her silhouette appeared at the bedroom door, in a white nightdress down to her feet.

He touched her hands.

"How was it?" she asked.

"Fine. And you here? How are the children?"

"They're fine."

The hint of a cold made her voice seem even warmer.

"What's been happening around here?" he asked.

"The Veterans' Circle asked about you the day before yesterday," she said. "I don't know why."

"Anything new?"

"Anything new? All the smart people are talking about Ali Pasha's widow, Vasiliqia. They say that so far she's turned down two proposals. Still, Lady Makbule said yesterday that she's no great beauty."

"Hmm. Nothing else?"

"Nothing," she said. "Oh, yes, they say that things are not going well for Gizer, the minister."

"Really?"

"Jakup Pasha's daughter said so yesterday at the tailor's."

"Anyway, don't repeat that to anybody," he said, taking off his sheepskin cloak.

"Of course not," she said. "I've no need to say anything. Are you going to have a bath?"

"Yes."

"There's hot water in the bathhouse. I'll bring you fresh clothes."

As he closed his eyes under the trickling water, he imagined how she was getting ready too, slowly taking off her underwear, splashing her sex with sweet perfume, and then, smiling vaguely as people do when they think of someone's irrational fancies, sprinkling her bush with white powder.

Fine rain had started to fall as soon as the weather turned milder, and a huge crowd of people swarmed to the square to see the head of Hurshid Pasha, once the hero of the hour. Just a few days ago, everybody had been discussing, speculating, and arguing about him, to the point of jeopardizing friendships of two, five, or even sixteen years. All these debates and conjectures and squabbles focused entirely on the future career of the victorious pasha, whom some confidently appointed as the minister of war, others as governor of Rumelia, and others still, who were few in number but for this reason all the more stubborn, to the post of grand vizier. Of course, there were those who doubted he would rise to any of these posts and shook their heads in bewilderment, before finally supporting one of the widespread predictions that imagined Hurshid Pasha in one of many possible roles, but never in the Traitor's Niche.

A general dismay had reduced most of the people who thronged the square to a uniform state of mind, just as the unexpected change in the weather had made their faces more or less identical, with their reddened eyes, running noses, and sneezes. As always, among the crowd were journalists, the staff of foreign embassies, veiled women, and curious spectators of all kinds. The faces of this swarm were all turned towards the niche, and they trod on one another's feet while their elbows, knees, and legs jostled and their bodies were pressed together. The artist Sefer had come as usual to paint in front of the niche. The pushing crowd had bent the supports of his easel, which now resembled the spindly legs of a stork.

Beneath the niche, its new keeper stood motionless. He

was short, with thick eyebrows, and with a commonplace jaw whose square shape seemed duplicated by his shoulder blades and his entire body, also square under its cloak. His inspecting eyes ceaselessly surveyed the multitude. He had to stand on tiptoe to see what was happening in the middle of the crowd.

The café was full, as usual on such days. The proprietor, who reckoned according to "head days" and plain "days," went back and forth among the tables with his coffeepot, whose gleaming copper seemed to smile as discreetly as the man himself.

"What strange villains people are," he said, pouring a black trickle of coffee into the cup of a redheaded man who seemed inclined to conversation. The trickle paled and petered out into tiny drops, and the café owner, seeing his customer show no irritation, went on: "I've always said, ever since the government opened this hole in the wall, that it will never be left empty. For people are villains and there's no improving them." The proprietor again studied the face of his customer, who had started to sip his coffee. "People will always be rising up in rebellions. That's why we have the word *hothead*, and their heads will be cut off, and the crowds seeing them in the Traitor's Niche will say to themselves, no, I'll never do a thing like that. That's what they'll say . . . yet, as if the devil is at their elbow, the first thing they think of doing is precisely what they shouldn't. For instance, do you see that midget of a supervisor? He was appointed only a few days ago. Before him there was another one, called Abdulla."

"Really, and where did he go?" said the redhead, lifting his eyes to the proprietor. "He was tall and thin, if I'm not mistaken. He looked rather dignified."

"That's right," the café owner said. "I've known all the keepers of the niche, that one too. He sometimes used to come for coffee after work, over at that table in the corner. He looked wise and, as you put it, sir, dignified, but one day, only last Saturday, something terrible happened."

"Really?" said the customer, now genuinely interested in what the proprietor was telling him.

"It was very strange," the café owner went on. "While he was on duty, this quiet, pale man suddenly turned red in the face. The veins in his temples swelled like leeches, and he totally lost control of himself. He looked dreadful, drunk, and he climbed the ladder by the niche and started shouting at the crowd."

"Really," said the redhead again. "How incredible."

"But worst of all were the things he said," the café owner continued. "People clapped their hands over their ears, not to incriminate themselves with what they heard, and others ran away."

"What did he say?" the other man asked.

"Oh, sir, the things he said." The proprietor lowered his voice. "Disgusting things."

"Really?" said the other man.

"He abused the offices of state, the sacred monuments, everything, and then he yelled: I am a rebel, do you hear, cut off my head, cut it off and put it there. And he pointed to the niche."

"Amazing," said the redhead. "And what happened next, did they really cut off his head?"

The café owner paused a moment and looked at the other man in amazement.

"No, sir," he said in a lifeless voice. "Such a thing could never happen. The idea of being beheaded and put in the Traitor's Niche . . . that was his own conceited fancy. There was no way that could happen."

"So what did they do to him?" the other man asked impatiently. "I doubt they gave him a medal."

"Of course not," said the café owner. "He was punished according to the law. But not beheaded or put in the niche. That would have been against all the rules."

"So what happened in the end?"

The café owner smiled. "In the end? That's simple, sir. They carry rebels of this kind, little rebels as they call them, to the swamp of Avdi Batak. Do you know this swamp, west of the city? They garrotted him with wire there, at the edge of that swamp."

"Ah, yes, I've heard of it, but I thought they took only adulterous wives there."

"They take those women there too," said the café owner, "as well as all sorts of other guilty people. They're all listed in the official gazette."

"Extraordinary, really."

"People are villains by nature," the café owner continued, but suddenly broke off as if someone had called for him. The voice was a soft squeak, like the creak of an ungreased pulley, which the proprietor's ear, to the other man's surprise, had caught at once. "I'm sorry, sir," he said, and with the coffee-pot in his hand he turned to the table where the former state criers were sitting as gloomily as ever.

Under the melancholy drizzle, the square was packed. The noise of the crowd echoed from the stone walls, like the roar of dark, heavy water behind a lock, the kind with levers and heavy iron gates below the surface.

As they stared at Hurshid Pasha's head, many people remembered Ali Tepelena. "So what happened to Black Ali's head? It was there until the day before yesterday, I saw it with my own eyes." "They say that bronze prices are on the move again." "Of course, of course, Ali Pasha's head. A dervish buried it on the outskirts of the city. His treasure was never discovered, or not all of it." "There's no way the bronze prices can change so soon. I heard about the hashish prices." "His treasure was never found, but there was nowhere he could hide his land. Hundreds of people have gone to measure it with rods, ropes, all kinds of tools and equipment. What an estate!" "There's some waste ground on the outskirts, under the old walls of Byzantium, and they buried the head there, a dreadful place."

The crowd had evidently knocked the legs of Sefer's easel again, and the artist's brush had slipped or his paints had spilled, leaving a fine loop just under the neck of the painted head. The spilled paint was black, and the mark resembled a trickle of dark blood belatedly dripping from Black Hurshid's severed head.

"Whose head is this?" a newcomer asked. Other people turned to him in surprise: "Where have you been hiding?" "Don't you read the papers?" "Don't you hear the criers? They've been shouting themselves hoarse since morning." Then the uproar became general. "Has the decree against Albania been published?" "No, I don't know anything. I listened to all the criers today when I came out of the office, but I didn't catch anything about Albania." "The army will take the situation in hand there." "I don't think so. They say that the military are rather angry. Whereas I heard . . . bring your ear a bit closer . . . that a dream arrived at the Tabir Saray yesterday evening, nobody knows where from . . ." "A dream?" "The interpreters have been analyzing it all night. Brr . . . it gives me the creeps." Late that afternoon the rain stopped, and towards evening a rainbow hung over the western part of the capital city.

At that hour of dusk the square was still full. The rumor was that a courier of the Tabir Saray had brought an important dream from the dusty margins of Anatolia. "What was that dream about, and what did it mean?" asked voices scattered throughout the square. Nobody could say. They knew only that the lights in the Palace of Dreams had burned until dawn. Someone said that they would carry the dream to the sovereign tomorrow. Apparently Albania's fate depended on it.

People turned their eyes in the direction where, they

thought, the emperor's winter palace must be, and shook their heads, as if wondering what this dream, which had arrived from so far away, might foretell.

On the square in front of the Traitor's Niche, the clamor continued unabated, striking deafeningly against the granite walls. That place again, so far away. Tell me again its name, as they call it themselves. *Shq* . . . *Shqe* . . . it's a name you can hardly pronounce. It's really hard, sticks in your throat. Its meaning is hard to understand too, I'm not really sure myself. *Shqip* . . . *Shqipre* . . . *Shqipëria*. A very difficult idea, a kind of convocation of eagles, with bloodstained feathers, that falls from the air, swooping through the storms, I don't know how to put it, oh Allah.

Tirana
1974–1976

ISMAIL KADARE is Albania's best-known novelist and poet. Translations of his novels have appeared in more than forty countries. He was awarded the inaugural Man Booker International Prize in 2005, and the Jerusalem Prize in 2015.

JOHN HODGSON studied at Cambridge and Newcastle and has taught at the universities of Prishtina and Tirana. This is the fifth novel by Ismail Kadare that he has translated.

Printed in the United States
by Baker & Taylor Publisher Services